The Adventures of

Sherlock Holmes

and the

Glamorous

Ghost

Book Two

Harry DeMaio

Hardcover 978-1-80424-048-9
Paperback ISBN 978-1-80424-049-6
ePub ISBN 978-1-80424-050-2
PDF ISBN 978-1-80424-051-9

Published by MX Publishing
335 Princess Park Manor, Royal Drive,
London, N11 3GX
www.mxpublishing.co.uk

Cover design Brian Belanger

Dedicated to GTP

A Most Extraordinary Bear

And to the late Ms. Woof

An Extremely Sweet

and Loving Dog

Acknowledgements

These stories have evolved over a long period of time and under a wide range of influences and circumstances. I am indebted to many people for helping to bring my versions of Holmes, Watson, Lady Juliet and Pookie to the printed and electronic page. Thanks most especially to my wife, Virginia, for her insights and clever suggestions as well as her unfailing enthusiasm for the project and patience with its author.

To Steve, Sharon and Timi Emecz for their outstanding support of my seventeen book Octavius Bear series and my Holmes pastiches. To Derrick and Brian Belanger for publishing The Glamorous Ghost Book One and several of my other Holmes and Solar Pons efforts. To Dan Andriacco, Amy Thomas, David Chamberlain, Jack Magan, and Gretchen Altabef for their enthusiastic encouragement. And to all of my generous Kickstarter backers.

To my sons, Mark and Andrew and their spouses, Cindy and Lorraine, for helping to make these stories more readable and audience friendly. To Cathy Hartnett, cheerleader-extraordinaire for her eagerness to see this alternate world take form.

Thanks also to Wikipedia for providing facts and specifics of Victorian England and elsewhere. And additional kudos to Brian Belanger for his wonderful illustrations and covers.

Obviously, these stories are tongue in cheek fantasies and require the reader to totally suspend disbelief. I do hope they are entertaining fun. I'm not sure what Heaven is really like but I hope to find out one day.

If, in spite of all this support, some errors or inconsistencies have crept through, the buck stops here. Needless to say, all of the characters, situations, and narratives are fictional. Some locations, devices, historical figures and events are real.

The Adventures of Sherlock Holmes

and the Glamorous Ghost

Book Two

Table of Contents

Prologue

She's Back! Welcome Lady Juliet Armstrong, Baroness Crestwell once again to our pages. A former sensation of the London musical stage; a feisty member of the British nobility by marriage but recently, a most definitely *deceased* arrival at the Elysian Fields. The obstreperous noblewoman was not content to don her halo and bland heavenly garb and join the other celestial denizens in eternal bliss. She had been shot and before going to her eternal reward she wanted to find the blighter who did it and bring him/her to justice. Who else to solve the mystery than Sherlock Holmes and Doctor Watson? Clad in her scarlet Parisian evening gown and wearing a chic corona fashionably tilted on her head, she persuaded the powers that be in Heaven to allow her to return to Earth and seek out Holmes' assistance. Thus began the first story in Book One of this collection of tales that takes the Glamorous Ghost, Holmes and Watson on a wild tour of crimes, personalities, situations and locations.

Holmes, no believer in ghosts, reluctantly acknowledged the noblewoman's otherworldly existence and agreed to cooperate with her in what has evolved into a series of semi-supernatural adventures. Watson followed suit.

Another ghostly and no less glamorous character aids and abets throughout. Pookie, a very clever and highly opinionated Bichon Frisé who predeceased her Baronial mistress, barks, whines and wags her way into the proceedings at every turn. Unruly as her owner, she is always instrumental in keeping the action going.

You will also meet Mr. Raymond, (a high ranking angel) who is the Senior Heavenly Director. One of his assignments is keeping the celestial environment under control. That includes Juliet and Pookie. No collection of Holmes stories would be complete without the Irregulars and they are here. Toby and Celeste, the wonder dogs are on hand with Mr. Sherman and a full complement of clever canines. Inspector Gregson and the wretched Athelney Jones make appearances. Major Philomena Monahan of the Salvation Army continues her good works. Many other characters fill these pages.

So now, in Book Two, the Baroness and her dog continue their fun-filled excursions from Paradise back to Earth with Holmes, the good Doctor and Mrs. Hudson, as well. Are you up for more madcap mystical mischief and mayhem? Join us!

The Garden Party – Command Performance

Lady Juliet Armstrong, Baroness Crestwell, had little time or inclination for garden parties or afternoon teas when she was alive in London. She eschewed the traditional performances and players: Mothers anxious to find suitable husbands for their debutante *(and often ugly)* daughters. Spouses being critically evaluated. Extra marital affairs discussed behind gloved hands or extended fans. The New Season analyzed and re-analyzed. Money, never discussed but always alluded to and the infernal pecking order – Duchess This lording *(ladying?)* it over Countess That or Marchioness Whoever.

When she did appear, Juliet was subjected to the full treatment – a former actress in the musical theatre *(horrors)*; a Baroness by marriage to an oafish Peer without a hereditary estate to her name *(Dear me!)*; Defiance of fashion demands *(She wears French scarlet gowns.)* and alliances with organizations that are beyond the pale. *(Suffragists, Work House Relief, Support for the Miners).* She was a social pariah but a wealthy pariah *(earnings from the stage and clever investments plus Reginald's income).* Therefore, she was just tolerated and grudgingly invited to events she really didn't want to attend. But needs must!

So when she was shot to death and transported to the Elysian Fields, the London Good and Great gave her a hypocritical farewell, buried her and promptly forgot her. Or at lease most of them did. In some circles, both Earthly and Above, Baroness Crestwell is a legend and continues to be one. She and her dog Pookie found themselves the center of attraction among the recently and not so recently deceased female denizens of the heavenly sanctums. In addition to her magnificent contralto performances in the Angelic Choir; her star turns in the Heavenly Theatre Guild's Saintly Spectaculars and incredible aerobatic flying skills, word had gotten around about her post mortem adventures with the famous detective Sherlock Holmes and his associate Doctor John Watson. She and Pookie were in great demand by the ghostly ladies looking for some excitement, however vicarious, in Heaven's sedate atmosphere.

So it was that Lady Juliet Armstrong and her extremely clever dog found themselves at a garden party in a delightful bower arranged by the UK branch of the Celestial Sisterhood. She had been a guest of the American, Canadian, Australian and Indian wings and was very much on call. This was her third meeting with the British group. Unlike the soirees and gatherings in the English homeland, the Sisterhood's garden parties were democratic in the extreme. Barmaids rubbed shoulders with baronesses. Shopgirls with society sisters. Young girls with elderly matrons. Bright young things *(the few that made it to Heaven)* Religious women with reformed prostitutes. A group of angels had also joined the party. All in a spirit of generosity and camaraderie. Such fun!

Because they were all ephemeral souls, convential gardem party fare – coffee, tea, cakes, sandwiches – were not on the menu BUT ambrosia and nectar were. The mythological food and drink of the gods, goddesses and spiritual beings. Animals, however, enjoyed their own nourishment. Pookie was polishing off a tasty Heavenly Chewy and was looking about for more. A few other pets were in attendance and she had just finished trying unsuccessfully to chase a cat. Oh, well! Bad habits die slowly.

One of the ladies had just related in lengthy detail her unfortunate demise on a ski slope. Tuts and expressions of sympathy for the victim who demurred. In fact, she said she was having the time of her *(after)* life slaloming under the Rainbow Bridge and behind the Pearly Gates. Laughter all around.

The Chair Lady, a rotating assignment, said, "Thank you, Miss Abernathy, for that most entertaining narration. It is now my

10

pleasure to introduce our very special guest of the celestial afternoon. Many of you know her from her sparkling appearances in the Saintly Spectaculars Revue presented by the Heavenly Theatre Guild. She is also a virtuoso performer with the Angelic Choir. And she and her dog are championship aerobatic fliers. But I'm afraid, Baroness, your unique fame depends in large part on your extraordinary relationship with the enigmatic consulting detective, Sherlock Holmes and his biographer and associate Doctor John Watson. Ladies, I give you Lady Juliet Armstrong, the former Baroness Crestwell, actress, adventurer, detective and unique traveler on Earth in ethereal form."

Soundless applause. *(Wraith-like hands clapping don't make noise.)* Juliet took a gulp of ambrosia and rose gracefully to the small platform. "Thank you, Madame Chairwoman. And thank you all for that gracious reception. I'm very pleased to be given the opportunity to meet groups like this and share my thoughts and adventures."

"I thought I would relate one of my theatrical experiences before launching into the information you all came here to learn about. Sherlock Holmes? Am I right? *(More soundless applause.)* Just be patient as I tell you about my last performance as an ingenue in the production of 'Jolly Juliet' at the Palladium. I had been playing to packed houses for which I was most grateful but all things terrestrial come to an end, as all of us here know."*(Polite laughter)*

"Baron Reginald Crestwell had proposed marriage and in a fit of youthful foolishness, I agreed, putting an end to my career as a thespian. On the night of my final performnce as Juliet Armstrong before taking up the new role of Baroness Crestwell, a woman, Selma Fairfax by name, stormed backstage and accused me of stealing her husband-to-be. I was dumbstruck and watched open-mouthed as two brawny members of the cast helped her, none too gently, to exit the theatre. I confronted Reginald who swore he knew nothing about it or her. I stupidly believed him and we proceeded to our nuptials. One year later, on returning from dinner, the Baron and I were attacked by two absurd triggermen. He was wounded. I was killed. The police assumed he was the target and I was collateral damage. Silly them!"

"On reaching the Pearly Gates, I refused to enter, giving our beloved Director Raymond a terrible time. I insisted I would join Elysium only after I had discovered who it was that had arranged to have me assassinated. Finally Raymond relented and allowed me to return to Earth."

"Here is that discussion." Juliet skillfully mimicked Raymond: 'Well, Baroness, It's highly unusual but I suppose I could invoke Loophole M and allow you to contact one individual. Only one, mind you. And only for five Earth days. That's the extent of my flexibility. Otherwise, I shall have to summon an archangel or two. Now, what's it to be and who's it be?' "

"Why, that's easy, you silly git! Sherlock Holmes, of course!" *(Laughter and applause.)*

"That's how I first met the Great Consulting Detective."

A voice from the second row. "Coo, Milady. Who did you in?"

She laughed, "Two goons hired by- are you ready for this?- Selma Fairfax."

("Ooohs")

"It seems dear Selma was in the employ of a foreign spy and was using Reginald as a source of strategic information. He was with the Foreign Office at the time and had a terribly big mouth.

12

Selma had been using her feminine wiles and was reporting back on his braggadocio. By marrying Reggie, I had unwittingly cut her off at the pass and dried up her access. Both she and her employer decided I needed to be eliminated. They hired the gunmen and that was the end of my earthly self. As a spirit, I approached Holmes who was loath to deal with women or believe in ghosts but nevertheless finally took me on as a partner and we brought the two of them to justice. The spy escaped but Selma was hung for my murder. I don't know where she is but it isn't here." *(laughter)*

"Now let's take on the question all of you want to ask. Just who is Sherlock Holmes? Answer: I don't really know and neither do any of his associates – Doctor Watson; Mrs. Hudson, his landlady; the detectives of Scotland Yard; his Irregulars. I suspect the Dog Toby may have some insights." Pookie stirred and barked her approval.

"Perhaps the one who knows him best or is equal to Watson in that regard is his brother Mycroft Holmes. He too is a very elusive but unbelievably intelligent individual. They are a daunting pair."

A gentle voice from the back of the room *(An angel?)* "Can you share some of your adventures with Mr. Holmes?"

"I will in just a moment but let me describe him and Watson first. To understand some of our adventures, you need some understanding of Holmes the man, to the extent I can supply it."

She smiled. "His intellect, energy and self-regard are formidable or even more so."

"When I first approached him, he stated categorically, *"This agency stands flat-footed upon the ground and there it must remain. No ghosts need apply."* He has since changed his mind. *(Laughter)*

Another voice commented. "I have heard he has a low opinion of women. How did you handle that?"

"I'm not sure. Just plain persistence and competence, I suppose. He views women as unfathomable and not always trustworthy. There are several women who have been exceptions:"

"Irene Adler is a retired American opera singer and actress. I assume she's still alive. She seems to be the only woman to match him intellectually. Holmes holds her in a high regard although not to the point of love. But she is '*The Woman*' in his eyes."

"Mrs. Hudson is Sherlock Holmes' and **Doctor Watson's** landlady. Holmes tests her patience with his clutter, malodorous scientific experiments, ill-timed musical outbursts, and the strange individuals who steadily visit him. But she is overwhelmed and is actually quite fond of him. Oddly, Holmes can be a consummate gentleman and exhibit remarkable courtesy when dealing with women. He is a puzzlement."

She continued, "Mary Morstan, now deceased, was the wife of Doctor Watson."

An attractive brunette rose from her seat. "I am here, Lady Juliet." This set off a spate of murmurings in the audience.

Retaining the aplomb for which she was famous, the Baroness nodded and invited her to come up to the podium.

"Welcome Mrs. Watson. If I'd known you were here I would have invited you to join me immediately. The floor is yours. You are much more qualified to speak of your relationship with Holmes and of course to describe Doctor Watson to us."

"Thank you! I didn't mean to interrupt your most perceptive and entertaining presentation but I can make a few comments. I originally was a client of Sherlock Holmes. Ours was a strained relationship from the start although he was always a gracious gentleman. I'm certain that Holmes resented me a bit when I later married his dear friend. My John Watson. If Holmes has regard for any women it is because they demonstrate intelligence, bravery, trustworthiness, creativity, and composure. That certainly describes you, Baroness. Perhaps I fit somewhere in that category too. "

Juliet responded, "I'm sure you do and thank you for the kind words but please, tell us about your husband. I have worked with him. You lived with him."

"John Watson lives in the shadow of the Great Consulting Detective but he is hardly a cipher. He is intelligent, perceptive, extremely brave, incredibly loyal, thick-skinned, gentle and genteel, an excellent physician and of course, a remarkably fine writer. His stories have propelled Holmes into the public limelight and I assume, enhanced the size and quality of his clientele. I am so proud to have been John's wife and so look forward to him joining me again. Thank you."

She descended gracefully from the podium and reclaimed her seat. Among the audience, tears flowed. Unusual in the realm of joy and delight. After a short pause, the Baroness resumed, wiping her own cheeks.

"Well, I promised you an adventure story and I will not disappoint. This is one that has not been recorded by Doctor Watson. I doubt if it ever will see the light of day."

That stirred her listeners and they leaned forward attentively. She noticed that Director Raymond had slipped covertly into the bower. She wondered to herself, "Is he checking up on me. Fear not, Raymond. The truth, the whole truth and nothing but the truth."

Just as she was about to begin her narrative, a sharp bark echoed amid the participants. A glassy-eyed Pookie had found an unguarded bowl of nectar and had slurped it down. She alternated licking her chops and hiccupping. The Bearoness who was used to the Bichon providing comic relief chose to ignore her canine

15

associate whose halo had slipped into an even more precarious position than usual.

"I call this tale Command Performance. It involved Britain's lately deceased Queen and Empress. You know that I have always been theatrically involved. While it has been said by Doctor Watson and others that Holmes would have made a wonderful actor since he is a consummate master of disguise, oddly enough, he is not a very skillful singer. In this adventure, he was called upon to be one."

"He was quite aware that he needed a voice coach and while he is well acquainted with members of the Musical Stage, the confidential nature of this particular case was such that he could not call upon their expertise. Who could he consult who had the necessary experience and ability but would not, nay *could* not, reveal the story to the public? Why, someone who was dead, of course. Namely me. I have no hesitation in passing on my story to all of you for you share my condition but it never will be circulated among the living. Yes, I know you think I'm being evasive or coy at the moment. I shall remedy that immediately."

"Of course, you are all familiar with Windsor Castle. I'm sure some of you visited it or even lived there at one time or another. *(Nodding Heads)* Queen Victoria and Prince Albert made Windsor Castle their principal royal residence, disdaining Buckingham Palace. Windsor reached its social peak during the Victorian era, with invitations to numerous prominent figures to "dine and sleep" at the castle."

"Victoria was always an enthusiastic patron of the theatre and opera, favoring popular and even lowbrow performances. She was a frequent visitor to the London theatres. She adored Gilbert and Sullivan. This activity stopped with the death of Prince Albert. In her extreme mourning, she never again visited a playhouse."

"But towards the end of her reign, plays, operas, and other entertainments slowly began to resume at Windsor castle. *(I never had the opportunity to entertain her prior to her recent passing.)* Our story of an attempted assassination of the Queen is based on one of those offerings. *(Rapid intake of breath by the audience.)* It involved Messer's Gilbert and Sullivan's comic opera The Mikado."

"The Foreign and Home Offices had received an anonymous tip that an attempt on the Queen's life would be made during the performance of that opera at the Castle. First reaction was to withdraw the presentation but the Lord Chamberlain felt the Queen would be greatly annoyed at the cancellation. Any mention of a potential threat would just strengthen her insistence that the show must go on. High ranking members of the Royal Household approached Mycroft Holmes who after consultation with the Home Office, Foreign Office and Scotland Yard came up with a plan. Insert Sherlock Holmes into the Mikado cast and let him use his impressive powers to identify and overcome the assassin."

"Holmes was torn. First and foremost, he was pledged to defend the Sovereign but, splendid actor that he was, his singing voice was, to be kind, sub-par. He had only two weeks to remedy the situation. To make matters worse, D'Oyly Carte had assigned him the leading role of Ko-Ko, ironically the Lord High Executioner. He acquiesced and in a moment of typical genius, he sought aid of a peculiar sort. Me!"

"As I'm sure you know, I sing!" *(Laughter)* "I'm sure some denizens of Heaven wish I would shut up. But my years on the Musical stage plus my deceased condition made me the ideal choice to be his coach. Besides, in my younger days, I played the ingenue part of Yum-Yum and was quite familiar with the story line and score of the Mikado."

"Director Raymond is in the back of the bower. *(Turning heads! Some giggles!)* I'm sure he will attest to the fact that Holmes contacted the Pearly Gates to solicit my aid on behalf of the British Sovereign."

Raymond, unusual for him, seemed bewildered. Although, when he was perplexed, his upset was usually caused by the Baroness. Juliet's trips to Earth were strictly confidential and here she was, spilling the celestial beans. A follow-up conversation between them would be required. He recovered his composure and nodded agreement. "Mr. Holmes maintains contact with us and did indeed seek your assistance. A journey to Earth was approved for you and your dog."

Pookie picked up on the word 'dog' and did a series of graceful leaps to the delight of the audience. Her halo bounced on the floor. Amid gales of laughter, Lady Juliet recovered the ring and plopped it back on the dog's head feeding her a Heavenly Chewy in the process. She looked to the back of the area. "Thank you, Mr. Raymond. I appreciate the confirmation."

"So it was that Pookie and I made yet another journey down to London and 221B Baker Street. How many of you have read Doctor Watson's stories?"

Most hands went up. A young girl sighed. "I never learned to read until I died and went to Heaven."

An older woman had passed on before Holmes, Watson and Juliet were born. The rest had read the books. That's why they were at this event.

"Well, then I don't have to spend much time describing their living quarters and arrangements. Comfortable chaos kept in check by Mrs. Hudson, bless her. Holmes and Watson were awaiting our arrival."

"*Welcome, Milady and Pookie,*" he said, "*it seems I am in need of some musical tutoring. My skills on the strings of my violin do not translate to my vocal cords.* Watson, I suggest you retire to your club while the Baroness and I go through the agony of singing scales and rehearsing the role of Ko-Ko, the Lord High Executioner. Perhaps you would like to take Mrs. Hudson out to tea?"

"Watson mimed holding his ears and left in search of their landlady."

I asked, "*Before we begin our exercises, suppose you tell me what this is all about.*"

"*Top secret! The authorities have received an anonymous tip that an assassination attempt will be made on the Queen Empress during a presentation of Gilbert and Sullivan's Mikado at Windsor Castle.*"

"*That's easy! Cancel the performance!*"

"*The Queen would not hear of a cancellation. She has not been informed that she is in danger. Actually, we want it to go on so we can capture the potential killer in the act. I have been assigned that task. In the past the Queen has been an aficionado and knowledgeable critic of light opera.*"

"*Wouldn't she recognize you? You have performed a number of services for her..*"

"*Not disguised as a Japanese courtier but she certainly would not approve of my untrained voice. Hence my need of your vocal and theatrical skills. The game is afoot, Baroness.*"

"And so it was, ladies. Holmes was determined to raise his vocal abilities to near-opera level in two weeks' time. Frankly, I was dubious but I had underestimated Holmes in the past and so we began our work in earnest. Day followed day. Being ethereal, I was not subject to exhaustion but Holmes clearly became tired and often frustrated. Pookie hid under the sofa, paws to her ears. However, we made progress. "Behold the Lord High Executioner" and "Willow, Tit-Willow" went from audibly unbearable to actually quite pleasant."

"We also rehearsed his part with me playing all the female characters and Watson as the male courtiers. It's a shame we couldn't take our slap-up production on the stage. It was quite entertaining in a bizarre way."

"Meanwhile, the authorities were searching for more clues to confirm the anonymous report they had received. We were summoned to the Diogenes Club by Mycroft who is aware of my existence. He doesn't approve but who cares."

"The Diogenes Club with its incommunicado denizens is one of my favorite locales for exercising unseen hi-jinks. I have to restrain Pookie from relieving herself on the rugs. Of course, her output is evanescent so no terrestrial harm would be done. I entertain myself by making fun of the Major-domo and Desk Clerk and also making faces at the members hidden in their silence behind newspapers and books. I also check to see if they are alive. Childish? Of course!"

"Holmes and Watson were ensconced in the Stranger's Room awaiting Mycroft's arrival. Pookie and I flitted into the chamber in our best Celestial Flying School form and landed on a side table. She barked at the unattainable bowl of Turkish Delights kept at the ready for Mycroft. I gave her a Heavenly Chewy to assuage her constant hunger."

"Holmes started the conversation when Mycroft arrived. 'There are twenty two members of the Mikado cast including the choruses. That doesn't include the director, stage hands or members of the orchestra. Can you narrow down the list of suspects? I assume there will also be members of the Imperial Household and guards in attendance. I am sure Richard D'Oyly Carte, Sir Arthur Sullivan and Sir William Gilbert will be there to be greeted by the Queen and hear me torture their work. It must have taken immense pressure to get them to permit me to play Ko-Ko. Has your anonymous informant been any more enlightening?'"

"Mycroft shrugged, 'Another letter. This time on Windsor Palace stationery. We are trying to trace the handwriting. No luck yet. Once again warning that the Queen will be victimized by an assassin on the night of the performance. We are taking the information seriously. How are your singing lessons progressing?'"

"Holmes shrugged in return. 'The role calls for a comic baritone. Until a few days ago, it was all comic and no baritone but with patient confidential coaching, I am beginning to sound respectable. Fortunately, there will be no theatre critics in the audience.'"

I laughed, "*None except the Queen, Holmes. She is demanding and not easily amused.*"

"Holmes thanked me profusely for my encouragement."

"Our lessons, drills and rehearsals went on and Holmes was now giving a creditable performance as Ko-Ko. Pookie no longer hid under the sofa and Watson who had transmuted into a varied cast of Japanese gentlemen, applauded."

"I looked at Holmes. '*Has it occurred to you that you are probably a foot taller than anyone else in the cast?*'"

"*Some cast members wear elevated shoes. I shall not stick out.*"

"*Let us hope not. Do you have any idea who the potential assassin is?*"

"Holmes laughed and sang telepathically, *'I've got a little list.'"*

"Very funny, Holmes!"

*****

"The dress rehearsal went as all dress rehearsals go. Sporadic, repetitive, error-filled, emotional, troublesome but finally concluded. D'Oyly Carte, Sullivan and Gilbert were all in attendance. Several times, one or the other of them threw up his hands in despair and threatened to cancel the production. Oddly, Holmes was not the source of most of the irritation. Once again, they were reminded that the Queen would be most displeased if the performance did not come off. Reluctantly, it was decided that the show must go on. Or in Holmes-speak, the game was afoot."

"Members of the cast wondered who this newcomer was playing Ko-Ko and a story was concocted that the choice was the Queen's. Who was going to question Victoria? Raised eyebrows persisted but Holmes managed to carry his weight and then some. His "Tit-Willow" was quite effective. I wondered whether he had been bitten by the stage bug. It would be interesting to watch him tread the boards in future productions. It has never happened. At least, not so far!"

"The night finally arrived. The stage had been erected, the scenery installed, the orchestra secure in their places. There had been a minor last minute issue with a few missing props and one costume mishap but the characters were all in readiness. A number of plain clothes policemen as well as members of the military were posted around the ballroom but this was as expected whenever the Queen was to be in attendance surrounded by outsiders. Their numbers had been increased because of the anonymous tip. The room had recently been upgraded to electric lights and several limelights were also available for use during the performance. Two

22

members of the military were carrying out last minute searches for weapons, explosives or other dangerous objects. They found nothing. Watson was seated two rows behind the seats for the Royal entourage. Pookie and I took unseen positions stage right and left."

"The lights dimmed and a drum roll followed by a cymbal crash introduced an orchestral rendition of 'Britannia, Rule the Waves.' The audience rose and joined in singing the rousing melody. Applause at the conclusion. A brief moment of silence and then another drum roll preceded the familiar strains of 'God Save The Queen.' The lights went up and The Queen/Empress slowly entered the room leading her entourage to the sounds of the national anthem being lustily sung by all and sundry. I'm sure the lyrics struck Holmes, the Chancellor, Mycroft, Watson, D'Oyly Carte, Gilbert, Sullivan and the members of law enforcement as urgently paradoxical considering the situation. God Save the _Threatened_ Queen, indeed! Where was the assassin? When would he or she strike? How? Would Holmes and the officers of the law be swift and skilled enough to prevent disaster? Pookie and I sat invisible at our posts on either side of the stage, alert to spot any intrusion."

"Once the Queen had seated herself in her throne-like chair, the audience followed suit. The house lights dimmed once again. The limelights flooded the curtain as it slowly parted on the town of Titipu. The chorus of nobles emerged and sang: 'If you want to know who we are. We are gentlemen of Japan…'

"Yes,' I wondered, 'but is one of you an assassin?'"

"The first act proceeded in fine theatrical fashion. Holmes acquitted himself quite well in his tongue-in-cheek role of Ko-Ko, the Lord High Executioner. The irony of his role was not wasted on those of us who knew his real purpose in being in the comic opera. The act ended and the Queen rose and proceeded through a side door to a nearby withdrawing room accompanied by her ladies-in-waiting , the Security Officer and several guards. D'Oyly Carte, Gilbert and Sullivan joined them. I would have held my breath if I had any for I believed this was where and when the cowardly deed would be carried out. Could the ladies and the guards be trusted? Where was Holmes? To my surprise, I discovered he had done a quick change of costume and went into the withdrawing room dressed as a guard."

"The interval ended when the Queen decided to resume her seat unharmed and unaffected. She was theatrically savvy and knew enough to leave time for scenery adjustments, costume changes and prop replacements to take place backstage. She seemed to be enjoying the performance, laughed and clapped her hands at appropriate spots and even nodded her head and tapped her feet to the music. I'm not sure but I believe she even sang along at one or two points. *(Contrary to the usual reports, she WAS amused.)* If she had any inkling of a plot being hatched, she showed no sign."

"Act Two began and progressed as written. Holmes had managed to reappear as Ko-Ko without missing a beat. 'Here's a howdy-do.' sang the trio and it seemed to sum up the situation. Nothing yet had happened. The opera came to a close after its typical comic to's and fro's, misunderstandings, ridiculous explanations, inane decisions and happily-ever-after solutions. Amid resounding applause, the Queen rose and the orchestra played the national anthem once again. Had God Saved Our Gracious Queen once more? It seemed so."

"After the audience withdrew for late evening refreshments, the law authorities gathered as a frustrated group. Indeed, nothing had happened! Was the whole thing a cleverly executed hoax to create consternation among the guardians of Her Majesty? Had the presence of the police, military and private detectives panicked the prospective assassin? Any attempt would have been suicidal but that was typical of regicides. A conference was called for the next morning in Mycroft Holmes' office."

"I approached Holmes, *'Well, that was a refreshing evening of theatre but an unexciting ending. At least, your singing voice has improved immensely. Are you ready for a new career on the stage?'*"

"*No Milady, I am not. Thank you for all of your assistance. If you and Pookie want to return to your heavenly quarters, please feel free. But this isn't over yet*"

"*What do you mean?*"

"*This was no hoax.*"

*****

"Well, ladies, he was right. At 3 AM the following morning, an explosion erupted in the ballroom at Windsor Castle where the opera had been performed. The movable stage was totally demolished, windows were shattered by the concussion, chairs were broken and hurled all about the room. One door was torn from its hinges. Fortunately, no one was in the room or the adjoining corridors at the time. Mercifully, nothing caught fire. The Castle Security Unit and Fire Brigade were awakened and took charge of containing the damage, determining the cause and assuring that no additional explosives were at hand. They concluded that a bomb had been lodged under the front of the portable stage. If it had gone off during the performance, the actors, orchestra and the Royal party all would have been killed or seriously injured. Including the Queen!"

"The press found out and swarmed both the Castle and Whitehall interviewing all in sight and attempting to view the actual damage. A cordon of constables and soldiers kept them at bay."

"The planned meeting at Mycroft's office was rapidly set in motion. Members of the Home and Foreign Offices, Scotland Yard, the military and the Queen's senior staff all tried unsuccessfully to squeeze into the confined space and the session was moved to a larger conference room. Mycroft chaired the session. Both Sherlock Holmes and Doctor Watson were prominently in attendance. Pookie and I sat invisibly on a sideboard. We weren't going back to the Elysian Fields anytime soon."

"Mycroft called the meeting to order. 'A few miscellaneous items before we take up the major issue. First, Her Majesty is aware of the calamity and is her stoic self. She and her retinue have been transported from Windsor to Buckingham Palace where they are under a strong protective watch. Second. A special session of both Houses of Parliament has been called and the Prime Minister in engaged in managing that event. While Mr. Cecil would much prefer to be at this meeting, politics dominate. He has sent his Deputy who will be joining us shortly. Third, The Metropolitan Police are rounding up acknowledged foreign agents, Irish Fenians, anarchists, dissidents, protestors and other groups known for their use of explosive devices.' "

" 'Now,' he said, 'let us turn our attention to the event itself. How did it happen?'"

"The Queen's Chancellor cleared his throat and with a face that matched my scarlet gown said, 'The military team that we had commissioned to search for weapons and explosives did not check under the portable stage. The proscenium, scenery and props were in place and it was deemed too heavy and clumsy to move. An obvious error on their part.' "

"Holmes asked, 'Were there any remnants of the bomb found at the scene? I am especially interested in any clockwork mechanism that may have been used to ignite the fuse.' "

The Chief of Castle Security responded. 'We found what looked like some form of mechanical timer in pieces under the wreckage. Too fractured and scattered to provide any coherent clues.' "

"Holmes replied, 'It is too early to reach a definite conclusion but I would surmise that the timing of the device was set in error. It should have gone off during the performance. I don't believe simply doing damage to the ballroom during the early morning hours was the intent. From the warnings we received, it seems likely the Queen was the target and the cast and her retinue were regarded as expendable collateral damage.' "

"I winced, Ladies. My death was deemed 'collateral damage' by Scotland Yard as part of an assassination attempt on my then husband. They were wrong. I was the primary target. That term is so cold and uncaring. A life is a life. No one is expendable."

Her audience agreed and once more silently applauded.

"The meeting went on. The Home Secretary asked, 'Who could have planted the device? Who constructed the stage and set it up? Have we fully analyzed the threatening letters? Mr. Holmes, we want you, Inspector Gregson of Scotland Yard and Colonel Jeffers of the Army to form an independent panel of inquiry.' He turned to the Chancellor and the Chief of Castle Security. 'Gentlemen, I'm sorry but since you were directly involved in implementing the opera's logistics and protective measures, you do not have the independence required to be part of this panel. I make the exception for Mr. Sherlock Holmes who was hired based on his investigative experience and disinterested participation in pursuing an attempt on Her Majesty's life. I expect you to give this panel your fullest cooperation.' "

"The Deputy Prime Minister had arrived and on Mr. Cecil's behalf approved the plan with the somewhat unnecessary comment that time was of the essence. The government must be seen by the Queen and public to be dealing with this horrendous affair with all due dispatch and the fullest resources. Holmes now found himself with a very substantial monkey on his back and only a modicum of investigative skill from the other members of the panel. Colonel Jeffers was an infantry line officer and Gregson, well, Gregson was Gregson. Holmes turned to Watson, Pookie and myself and telepathically said, *'Your assistance is required. Let us repair to Windsor Castle and examine the site ourselves.'"*

"He turned to Gregson and the Colonel and suggested they return with him to the scene of the crime. He asked the Castle Chief of Security, Major Smithers to accompany them. Mycroft adjourned the meeting and set a return session for two days hence."

"Pookie and I flitted to the Windsor ballroom and were engaged in examining the wreckage when our corporeal companions arrived. Since the dog and I were both ephemeral, there was no way we could upset the evidence. Holmes asked psychically, *'Have you discovered anything?'*

"The Bichon barked invisibly and inaudibly and set about scratching at the door to the Queen's withdrawing room. She ran back to the remnants of the stage and the bomb fragments and then ran once again to the door. Holmes, Watson and I watched her while Gregson, the Colonel and Major roamed around the ballroom stepping over glass and broken chairs. I said, *'Pookie, what is it?'* The dog whined and danced in front of the door and then, evanescent as she was, sprang through it."

"I followed her. Holmes opened the door and he and Watson walked through. A few chairs were tumbled over from the impact next door and several wine bottles were on the floor but otherwise there was no serious damage. The castle walls and the thick portal had withstood the blast. Pookie was circling a chair, sniffing and whining. Tail wagging wildly, she raced back out into the ballroom and planted herself on top of the bomb pieces. The message was clear. Whoever had set the explosives had been one of the attendants or participants who occupied the withdrawing room during the interval."

"Holmes turned to Major Smithers and said, 'We need a list of all those who accompanied the Queen to the withdrawing room during the interval. Of course, I was there as were you, Major, as Chief of Security. The Chancellor was also there along with many Ladies in Waiting. Please identify them. If my memory serves, D'Oyly Carte, Sullivan and Gilbert were also in attendance. I have reason to believe that one of those present were involved in placing the bomb. *(Of course, he didn't mention Pookie's anxious behavior.)* Also. get a list of the domestics who were serving the refreshments.' "

"Major Smithers replied, 'I say, Mister Holmes. That's a bit of a stretch. All those you've mentioned are above reproach, even the footmen and servers. Are you seriously suggesting that during the performance one of them intended a suicidal attempt to murder the Queen, her retinue and the opera cast and orchestra? I suggest we question the carpenters and craftsmen who constructed the stage. There may be a labor dissident among them. Scotland Yard has rounded them up already, have they not, Inspector Gregson?' "

"The Inspector nodded."

"I intervened, *'Pay no attention to him, Holmes. I trust Pookie. She may not be the tracking genius your Toby is but she is ultra-reliable. If she is connecting the bomb maker to a chair in the withdrawing room, believe her.'"

"The Bichon barked to emphasize my statement."

"Holmes replied telepathically. *'I have no doubt, Baroness and Pookie, but there are probably several culprits involved here. We need to uncover the entire plot. I am going to let this play out. I will insist that the Major do as I ask while we allow the police to*

*strongly interview their suspects and the team that built the stage.'
"*

"I bowed to his judgement."

"The Major went off to create his list beginning with the servers and then the Ladies in Waiting.

"As some of you know, a Lady in Waiting or court lady is a female personal assistant, attending the Queen. Some of you here today may have held the rank."

A few hands were raised. The Baroness went on "A Lady of the Bedchamber is the highest level of lady in waiting. Mistress of the Robes is the senior lady in the Royal Household. While she is responsible for the queen's clothes and jewelry, the post also has the responsibility for arranging the Rota of Attendance of the ladies, along with various duties at state ceremonies. Maids of Honour are the lowest level. These are essentially unmarried women. With their lesser unmarried status comes lesser rank and duties."

"While the Major was constructing his list of drawing room attendees and the military explosives experts were sorting through the wreckage, Holmes sought out the Queen's Mistress of Robes. Unfortunately, she was with the monarch at Buckingham Palace. A new Army staff car recently added to the Windsor Castle transport pool was called out by Colonel Jeffers. Holmes, Gregson, the Colonel, Major and Watson squeezed together for the hour long ride. Pookie and I swiftly flitted across the fields, estates and tightly clustered row houses of suburban London and landed beyond the imposing gates of 'Buck House.' We entered the huge edifice that had fallen into relative disuse since Victoria had decided to stay in Windsor after Prince Albert's death. Now, of course, the Court was temporarily reassembling itself at the Buckingham site until the bomb-related problems were dealt with."

"The Queen's Mistress of the Robes is Lady Louisa Montagu Douglas Scott, Duchess of Buccleuch and Queensberry, a long standing aide and associate of Her Majesty. Among her many roles, she schedules the assignments and duties of the Ladies in Waiting. Holmes was eager to seek her out to determine who was in attendance at the performance of the Mikado. Major Smithers requested an audience with her."

"They were shown into a well-furnished anteroom to await her arrival. Pookie and I took up positions on a sideboard."

"An attractive mother of eight, the Duchess among other things is an efficient administrator of many of the Queen's accounts. As Mistress of the Robes, she is the senior lady of the Court, directing the activities of Her Majesty's Ladies in Waiting. At the moment, along with the Chancellor, she was involved in arranging the Queen's transfer to Buckingham Palace. She arrived 'in full sail' accompanied by two countesses."

" 'Good afternoon, Major and Colonel. I am familiar with you, Mr. Holmes. Our most talented Ko-Ko. Her Majesty was quite taken with your performance. And you, sir! Am I correct that you are the famous Doctor Watson whose stories I so enjoy. You are a favorite among the Ladies of the Court.' "

"Watson blushed and I chuckled telepathically. *'Ask for a Knighthood, Doctor!'* She smiled and then said, "Well, to business. Needless to say we are near chaos at this moment and Her Majesty is not pleased with having to move. She would be less pleased if she were blown to pieces, of course. How can I help you?"

"The Major, Colonel and Holmes all started to speak. The detective deferred to the Security Officer. 'Milady, we are assembling a list of all the Royal Household who were present at last night's performance. We have the names of the guests, footmen and servers as well as the cast and crew of the Mikado, the orchestra

31

and the guards who were in the ballroom before and during the show. We do not have a complete roster of the Ladies in Waiting, however.' "

"Holmes intervened. 'I am especially interested in any of the ladies who did not return from the withdrawing room to the ballroom after the interval. Can you remember any such?'"

"The Duchess paused and took a sheet of paper from one of her companions. 'Thank you, Countess. Let's see. Everyone seems to be accounted for. Oh, wait. Lady Dorothea Forsythe. She's the daughter of Baron Forsythe. A Maid of Honour. When we were in the withdrawing room, she pled illness and asked to be excused from the remainder of the performance. I saw no reason to deny her request. The Queen was amply supplied with Ladies in Waiting.' "

"Holmes asked, 'May we speak to her?'"

"The Duchess looked at the Countess and asked, 'Is Lady Dorothea available and fit?'"

"'I will see, Milady. I believe she has moved here to the Palace. Excuse me! I will summon her.'"

"The Major turned to Holmes. 'I have several other inquiries I need to make, Mr. Holmes. I'm sure you, the Colonel, the Inspector and Doctor Watson can handle this yourselves.' He walked off."

" Watson remarked, 'I say, Holmes. He's a bit of a strange duck. Seems quite nervous although as Chief of Windsor Castle Security, having an explosion nearly wipe out the Queen and her entourage should be enough to unsettle anyone.'"

Gregson nodded in agreement.

"I looked at Pookie who, back at Windsor Castle had made her 'to and fro' excursions from the remains of the bomb to a chair in the withdrawing room. *'What do you think, girl?'* The dog whined and tapped her claws on the marble floor."

"I turned to Holmes and Watson. *'She's suspicious of our friend, the Major.'*"

"Holmes responded, '*So am I. Unfortunately, the way the furniture was disturbed and tossed about, it's impossible to say who was in that chair*. Ah, here comes the Countess with Lady Forsyth.'"

"Mr. Holmes, Inspector Gregson, Colonel Jeffers, Doctor Watson, may I introduce Lady Dorothea Forsythe, a Queen's Maid of Honour."

"Bow and curtsies all around."

"Faced with that formidable foursome, Lady Dorothea took on all the aspects of a frightened deer. Pookie looked at her, scratched her ear and flopped on the floor in front of the sideboard. No interest! The Maid of Honour had not occupied that chair."

"Holmes looked at the honourable noblewoman and asked, 'Are you quite recovered from your illness, Milady?'"

"She lowered her head and murmured, 'Yes, thank you, Mister Holmes. A bit of food poisoning, I believe. It came upon me suddenly during the interval. I'm sorry I missed the rest of the performance. I understand your act as Ko-Ko was quite charming. Perhaps you may be called upon again by Her Majesty to repeat it.'"

Watson asked, "Has the Royal Physician given you a full bill of help, Milady. I am a physician and would be happy to check your condition and make a recommendation."

" 'I did not see the Royal Physician. Everyone was so taken up with the opera, I did not want to make a fuss. I simply returned to my room and had a lie-down. Thank you for your offer, Doctor, but I am in fine condition. Countess, may I be excused? This transfer of the Queen has all of the Ladies in Waiting busy with assignments. I'm happy no one was injured by the explosion. What a terrible thing to have happened. Gentlemen, I don't suppose you know who is to blame.' "

"The Colonel responded, 'No, we do not, Lady Forsyth, but we will not rest until we have the scoundrels under lock and key. You and the ladies need have no fear. Buckingham Palace is well protected.' "

" 'I'm so glad to hear that. May I pass your comments on to the other ladies?"

" 'Of course. Please do and thank you for your time.'"

"She and the Countess walked off. Holmes turned to us and said, 'She's lying.' "

*****

In Heaven, the Garden Party audience sat in rapt attention, listening to Baroness Juliet weave her tale and Pookie wag her tail. Little had they realized that Queen Victoria, recently deceased, had come close to being assassinated along with her retinue in 1900. She actually died of a stroke at Osborne House on the Isle of Wight on 22 January 1901, at half past six in the evening, at the age of 81. The nation mourned her demise for an extended period.

Her spirit was welcomed through the Pearly Gates and it is said she has rejoined Prince Albert in an opulent celestial residence at an unidentified location. The intended deaths due to the explosion in 1900 were averted thanks to ineptitude on the part of the would-be assassin. Mr. Raymond was spared the preparations and greetings required for those members of the Court, the opera cast, orchestra, crew and the military and security members including Holmes and Doctor Watson who would have been entitled to cross over the Rainbow Bridge. Of course, some of them would have taken up residence in the nether regions. Lady Juliet chose not to mention that.

At that moment, Pookie, still feeling the effects of the ambrosia and nectar she had snarfed, burped loudly producing gales of laughter among the listeners. That same voice from the second row asked. "Coo, Milady. Who did the deed?"

"Patience, and I will tell you all."

"Who's Patience?"

More laughter!

*****

The Baroness continued her story. "Holmes turned to the rest of us. 'Where is the Major?'"

"No one knew. Supposedly, he was checking on the attendees but he was nowhere to be found. The Colonel checked with the Palace guards. He was last seen driving off the Palace grounds in the staff car."

"Holmes turned to Gregson. 'Have the constables track him down. Colonel, Let us recall Lady Dorothea. I want a sample of her handwriting."

"I smiled, *"Aha! You think she has written the anonymous notes. I knew there was something suspicious about her.'"*

"More likely, she <u>was</u> suspicious, Baroness. I believe she and the Major were having a relationship. He foolishly hinted at his plans and persuaded her to avoid the performance. She couldn't betray her lover but she also couldn't betray her Queen. Ha, here she comes with the countess.'"

"The Maid of Honour once again looked like a gazelle surrounded by a pride of lions (although lionesses are the more

35

dangerous.) I guess Pookie and I fulfilled that requirement. Of course, she didn't know about us. She looked at the Countess for support. That lady smiled gently but said nothing."

"Holmes looked at her and said, 'Lady Dorothea, I do not believe you were totally forthcoming with us when we met a few moments ago. Tell us about your association with Major Smithers.' "

"The blood rushed from the girl's face. 'What association, Mister Holmes? I know the Major as all of the Ladies in Waiting know him. He is in charge of Windsor Castle Security.' "

"'I believe your relationship goes a bit deeper than that, Milady. May I venture that you and the Major are having what is known as an affair?'"

"'Certainly not! How dare you? No such thing. I believe the Major is a married man. I am sorely offended and embarrassed at your assertion.' She looked at the countess who returned her gaze with a blank stare."

"I spoke to Holmes telepathically. *"Keep at it, Sherlock. She's lying. She is a lousy actress. Take it from a professional. There's something there.'"*

"Holmes nodded. "Lady Forsyth, We have reason to believe that the Major was involved in the explosion. (This was news to Gregson, the Colonel and Watson but not to Pookie and me.) We further believe that he warned you to leave the Windsor ballroom during the interval. The blast was supposed to take place during the second act. I have checked on the Major's background. He has had military experience commanding teams of sappers who use explosives to undermine fortifications. You were not taken ill. You staged an escape. Fortunately, the Major mistimed the bomb's clockwork but he had no opportunity to correct or cover his error. I believe you knew about his intentions and wrote anonymous warning notes to the Castle authorities. I shall require samples of your handwriting to confirm this.' "

"The Maid of Honour fainted. Watson grabbed her before she hit the floor and carried her over to a chair. The Countess assisted. He called for water and reaching into his bag brought out a tube of smelling salts and passed it under her nose. "

"She regained consciousness, coughed and tears ran down her face. Holmes was in no mood to be gentle. 'Did you or did you not send those anonymous letters warning of an assassination attempt on Her Majesty and her retinue?'"

"She coughed again, gulped and in a tiny voice, squeaked, 'Yes. Yes, I did. I could not stand by and watch regicide and slaughter being committed. I surely thought you clever detectives and military would stop him before he could succeed. I was wrong! I guess he mis-timed the explosion. Oh, I wish I were dead." She fell into a paroxysm of sobs.

"Holmes pressed on. 'Who is _he_?'"

"She looked up in wonder. 'The Major, of course. Didn't you know? I felt sure you suspected him.'"

" 'I did and now he has fled. Do you have any idea where he may have gone?' "

" 'He has a wife and two children in Croydon. He may have gone to them. Oh, I don't know.' "

" 'What was his motive?' "

"'Revenge! His nephew was an Army Officer too. He was dealing in stolen armaments and convicted of treason. He faced a firing squad. The family including the Major appealed to the Queen for clemency but she refused. She cited the deaths of our troops from the stolen weapons and allowed the sentence to be carried out. His nephew is dead and the Major was enraged. He swore retribution. That's when I panicked and wrote the letters. I loved him but I couldn't betray my Queen.' "

"She broke down again and moaned. 'What is to become of me?'"

"The Countess had called The Queen's Mistress of the Robes. Lady Louisa Montagu Douglas Scott, Duchess of Buccleuch and Queensberry looked at the Maid of Honour and said, "That will be up to the Queen. I cannot imagine you will be permitted to serve any longer as a Lady in Waiting. Do you gentlemen have any charges you wish to prefer against this woman? Inspector? General?' "

"Gregson replied, 'It doesn't seem she was involved in the actual plot and she tried to warn us. She would have been more convincing if she chose not to be anonymous but I feel no charges will be laid against her.' The general concurred. 'I agree. Of course the Major is a different matter. As soon as we catch him, he will join his infamous nephew.' "

"This led to another round of sobs on Lady Dorothea's part. 'Oh, What will father say?."

*****

In the heavenly bower. Lady Juliet paused her narration to allow her audience to react. Gasps, head shakes, a few tears. A former Lady in Waiting, now very much deceased, murmured. "That poor foolish girl."

Once again, the voice from the second row erupted. "Crikey, Baroness! Did they catch the blighter?"

Pookie barked. She jumped up on the podium and sat down next to her mistress, wagging her tail furiously. She wanted it known that she was a party to the story.

Juliet smiled, "Yes, dear, they know you spotted the Major first. Inspector Pookie on the job. My Wonder Dog."

This lightened the mood. The Baroness turned to the voice in the second row. "Yes, they did. He was captured trying to leave the country. It was his plan to die along with the Queen when the bomb went off. He would have been collateral damage, as they say. When that failed and he was trapped he was unwilling to face the disgrace of a firing squad and he shot himself."

"What about the Queen?"

"After the repairs were swiftly made, she returned to Windsor. She graciously thanked the participants but insisted that the story would never be told. The explosion was to be an accident. Ladies, if you should encounter the Queen here in Paradise, I suggest strongly that you do not refer to the incident. I am probably in trouble for telling it to you. But then, I'm always in trouble."

The Mystics of Evil

The perpetual heavenly sun beamed down on the celestial mansion of Lady Juliet Armstrong, Baroness Crestwell. A new day! But was it? It was difficult to measure days in eternity when darkness never descended on the Elysian landscape. She had no need for sleep so timelessness without end slipped by largely unnoticed. However, since she had been maintaining on and off contact with Sherlock Holmes and Doctor Watson back on Earth, she kept a little clock set to London Time and a Julian calendar of Earth days. An attempt to stay worldly while immersed in perpetuity. Her dog and constant companion, Pookie, had no such problems. She timed everything by the arrival of the next Heavenly Chewy snack.

The Baroness scratched the Bichon's ears. "All right, my girl. Time for a little exercise. Those treats are making you fat. Out we go. On to a romp in the Elysian Fields! And then, perhaps a bath!"

Pookie cocked an ear, tilted her head, yawned, licked her chops and having completed her little doggie ceremony, sat up and accepted her leash and collar. Not really necessary but strongly suggested by the Mansion Maintenance Council. Heavenly Bureaucracies! The bath was another subject altogether.

They rose and floated through the rooms of her ethereal chateau. Tastefully decorated in gold, silver and white but dominated by her signature scarlet, the celestial villa reflected her baronial cum theatrical personality. Gorgeous flowers bloomed eternally throughout the house, filling it with riotous color and otherworldly perfumes.

Heavenly Real Estate had done a marvelous job of designing and 'constructing' her perpetual home. With a flick of her evanescent fingers, she could change the colors, shapes, furnishings and dimensions of her property from small and cozy to boundless – all as the mood suited her. Each estate in Heaven took up no space at all but simultaneously stretched into infinity.

Equally, the dog could summon snug dens, grassy dells or sprawling expanses lined with restful cushions. Doggie toys and snacks were in abundance. Ghostly sheep, squirrels and cats appeared on order, ready to be chased. And Pookie, like her mistress, was a highly skilled aviator and winner of several Dog Fight Contests. Of course, baths were a bother. However, there was no cause for boring sameness or discomfort.

As she and Pookie emerged through the opaline glass doors she saw a figure she recognized all too well. She found herself facing an individual who had not been there a moment ago. A middle-aged male, tall, dressed in morning *(mourning?)* clothes, clean shaven, not a hair out of place, dark eyes, color undetermined. But, he seemed to be floating inches above the ground. Mr. Raymond, a Senior Celestial Director, charged with keeping Paradise in heavenly shape.

"Greetings, your ladyship. I trust you are well but how could you be otherwise here in Utopia. And Pookie. What mischief have you been up to?"

It wasn't clear if he was addressing the dog, the Baroness or both. Juliet's rebellious nature had given the Director bouts of agita in the past. Whether it was her insistence on eschewing the traditional white robes of the blessed for apparel of scarlet satin or her daredevil *(oops!)* flying techniques with the True Angels aerobatic team, Juliet and her dog were known to all as renegades. Add her travels back to Earth to participate with Holmes and Watson in crime-solving adventures, an activity slyly encouraged by the Almighty, and you had a singular mixture of virtue and roguishness. Pookie added further spice to the stew. Needless to say, Raymond, while pretending otherwise, was quite fond of both of them.

The Bichon barked, wagged her tail frantically and attempted to climb up his flawlessly tailored trousers. He reached down and ruffled her ears. The Baroness laughed. "I know you don't make social calls Raymond, so this must be in the way of some formal business. What infractions of celestial protocol are we guilty of this time?"

"Surprisingly, none to my knowledge, Baroness. Angelic Traffic Control has no outstanding citations. Pookie has stopped chasing St. Peter's squirrels and The Heavenly Theatre Guild is delighted with your performances in Saintly Spectaculars."

"Aha, so you must be here to beg a boon!"

"Got it in one, Milady. There is a problem in which the 'Powers That Be' would like you two to get involved along with your Earthside companions, Holmes and Watson."

"A commission from on high! How delightful. Tell me more!"

"As you are aware, the Almighty allows evil to exist on Earth for a number of reasons, not the least as a trial to allow humankind to work its way toward salvation."

"Yes. I know. I've experienced it. I sense there is a 'however' coming."

"Indeed. They draw the line when the reputations of redeemed beings who have been accepted in the Heavenly kingdom are being despoiled. We have had protests from the slandered and maligned souls here in Paradise. In London, a small group of so-called spiritists are pretending to establish contacts with the blessed to urge unwitting and superstitious mortals to commit crimes - thefts, assaults, even murders and assassinations. They call themselves The League of the Enlightened. We call them Mystics of Evil. Their mesmerized followers insist that through the League they have been instructed by the saints or gods to commit these outrageous acts. We want the League stopped and their practices destroyed."

"Wouldn't a few well-placed thunderbolts do the trick?"

"No, we want these villains to be subjected to human justice and exposed as the criminals they really are. Right now, they are posing as profound spiritual leaders commissioned by the saints and the Almighty to command and carry out their pernicious plots. Their deluded agents must be made to realize that they are deceived fools, dupes of these Mystics of Evil. Sherlock Holmes is the ideal person for this mission along, of course, with Doctor Watson, you and Pookie. Your evanescent state should be a great asset in bringing final closure to this disgraceful series of episodes."

Juliet looked at Pookie. "What do you think, girl? Want to see Holmes and Watson again?"

The Bichon barked, back-flipped, losing her halo, and shook her tail frantically. Another adventure!

*****

The chaotic sitting room at 221B Baker Street was inhabited by the usual suspects, each occupied in catching up on his reading and filling the area with clouds of smoke. A noiseless approach and Lady Juliet Armstrong stood shimmering in their midst. Not quite noiseless. Pookie barked telepathically and both Holmes and Watson, sensitized to their presence, dropped their newspapers and stared at the noblewoman and her canine.

Holmes reacted first, *"Ah, Baroness! And Pookie! I wondered if and when we would be seeing (or almost seeing) you two again. Thank you for arriving at a civilized time and not hauling us back from the sweet embrace of Morpheus."*

Watson smiled and said, *"Lady Juliet. Lovely as usual. Is that a new frock? Scarlet is indeed your color. And Pookie. You too look lovely. Welcome, both of you."*

"Thank you, Doctor. It's nice to know someone notices." She stuck her tongue out at Holmes.

The Consulting Detective grinned. *"I don't imagine this is a social call although your celestial presence is always welcome."*

"Correct! It is not. What a clever deduction. Have you considered a career as a detective? It might suit you better than what you do. Oh, enough badinage! As you suspect, I am here on a divinely directed mission. I believe you are familiar with a group called The League of the Enlightened or as they are known in Heaven, The Mystics of Evil. They prey on the foolish gullibility of superstitious individuals instructing them to commit crimes using influence and guidance from manufactured pseudo-saints, gods and even devils."

"Unfortunately yes, or should I say 'fortunately' for I am the only one equipped to deal with them."

"Careful, Mr. Holmes. Your humility is showing. There is outrage in Heaven over the false connection of the blessed spirits to the commission of crimes. They want it stopped and I have been sent to help and inspire you to end this debacle."

Holmes chuckled. *"Actually Baroness, I need little inspiration or support to deal with these miscreants. However, if your transcendent clients are so concerned, I am only too happy to accommodate your participation in this endeavor.* What say you, Watson?"

The Doctor responded. *"Always delighted to have another opportunity to work with Lady Juliet. Shall we compare notes?"*

Juliet looked at the two of them. *"What else do we know about this League of the Enlightened?"*

Holmes replied, *"They are elusive and quite small in number. They set themselves out for hire to "facilitate" felonious acts. Bespoke criminality! Paid in advance, they engage superstitious and fatuous individuals to do the actual dirty work. They concoct deceptive directions from the spirit world through seances, Tarot readings and pseudo religious ceremonies. It's a rather unusual but all too often, effective technique."*

"They are not just invoking pseudo saints. They are also known to prey on devil worshippers. You see, depending on the naïveté and gullibility of their potential agents, they pretend to call down the spirits of the virtuous, your heavenly colleagues, or they summon the minions of Satan from the circles of Hell. Equal opportunity. They do not discriminate. They tailor their messages and spirit messengers to the susceptibilities of their dupes who are predisposed toward spiritism. They want to believe and so they do. The League urges, or rather, commands them to do their outrageous bidding. They demand obedience and describe the crime and victim(s). Once the offense has been committed, the Mystics disappear and leave the perpetrators to fend for themselves with the police."

Juliet and Watson both looked perplexed. Pookie tilted her head and then scratched her nose.

The Baroness blew out her non-existent breath, *"That is the most bizarre and complicated process I have ever heard of. Since*

I've been involved with you two, I've had some pretty incredible experiences but this tops all."

Holmes laughed. *"I suppose you think solving crimes with two female ghosts, human and canine, is business as usual."*

"Touché. But I can't imagine being able to convince a true human believer in righteousness to commit a crime, especially something as heinous as murder."

"Milady. May I refer you to several such instances in the Bible? Do you think human sacrifice has been expunged from the religions of the world?"

"Yes, but those are barbarians! This is London. A bastion of civilization. At least sometimes."

Holmes chuckled, *"Have you forgotten how you were consigned to your immortal existence? I believe you were a deliberately targeted victim of an assassin's bullet. You and Pookie have helped us expose and defeat several murderers and a madman bent on destroying the world. To say nothing of thieves and kidnappers. Each showed a veneer of civilized behavior."*

"Baroness, I remember you once remarked that you were never shocked. Shocking, yes, but never shocked. Is that still true? (she nodded.) Good! I agree. But what they are doing is outré in the extreme. By the way, the crime is not always murder. There have been significant thefts, all in the name of social justice or revenge. Even a kidnapping or two."

Watson asked, "Have you been able to establish any identities?"

"The police have caught several of the perpetrators. They all tell the same story of otherworldly direction but no identification of the conspirators controlling their actions. Thus far we have been unable to snare the actual members of The League of the Enlightened or Baroness, as you refer to them, The Mystics of Evil. They are led by an individual who calls himself the Master. A woman initiates the first contact and conducts the seances or readings. We have no useful descriptions of either of them. They are mysterious and elusive. They hold their sessions in a variety of locations, never repeating. *Are you willing to participate in our chase, Milady? The assistance of a pair of highly motivated ghosts will be most welcome.*"

"Pookie and I are here under divine direction. Of course, we're willing. (The dog growled and rapidly wagged her voluminous tail.)

Watson laughed. *"We'll take that as a yes, Pookie. Good girl!"*

The Baroness looked at Holmes. *"All right, Sherlock. What's the plan?"*

"We infiltrate, Milady. We infiltrate."

"You mean we substitute real spirits for their fakes? Pookie and I?"

"Exactly! And we disrupt their malicious plots, But first we have to find them. I have a few ideas on that score."

"But as things are, Pookie and I can't be seen or heard by anyone except you and the good doctor. How can we defeat these villains if they're not aware of us?"

"Why don't you talk to Raymond and see what can be done about allowing you to become corporeal. Temporarily, of course."

"Heigh ho! Lady Juliet the actress will be on stage again along with her little dog. Back we go to the Pearly Gates, Pookie. Stand by, Holmes and Doctor!"

****

"Most unusual, Baroness, but since we commissioned you to take on this assignment, I can see the logic of your request. I'll have to seek authorization. Can't have you appearing and talking to every Tom, Dick and Harriet. You must proceed only in the line of duty, so to speak."

"Of course, Raymond. We don't want to go around frightening innocent souls. Now, we will have to be able to appear and disappear at will and use both our disembodied and physical limbs and voices. Actually, I think Pookie might enjoy chasing after flesh and blood cats or sheep. She's bored with the evanescent variety. Aren't you, girl."

Pookie yawned.

"None of that, Milady! Does the dog have to be an active apparition?"

"Oh yes! A snarling canine can be quite scary even if the sound is coming from a small, white furball. Her teeth are very effective."

"All right. I'll claim you need the capability in order to bring these Mystics of Evil to heel."

"And it will be true! Holmes is hatching a plan to deal with them. By the way, on Earth they call themselves the League of the Enlightened. Isn't that a classic? I'll be waiting, Raymond."

*****

Holmes and Watson were not idle while the Baroness was engaging in spirited negotiation in Heaven.

Holmes pondered, "I think we should volunteer to assist the Yard on this one. We need to interview the perpetrators they have in custody and learn all we can about the League of the Enlightened. Then, we can determine how best to organize our approach to meet with this so-called Master and his female mediator. I suspect I'll have to resort to a major disguise. You may too, Watson. Actually, you are less likely to be suspected of conspiring with the police. However, one unfortunate result of your incessant scribbling is I have become known to more and more of the criminal element. My masquerades usually are successful but it will be more useful if we have spiritists engaged in trying to attract the League's attention. What say you, old friend?"

"I suppose you are right, Holmes. It won't take much effort on my part to appear gullible."

"You are far too modest, my colleague. Let us approach Inspector Gregson and propose our participation but not let him in on our secret weapons from behind the Pearly Gates. The Baroness and her curly pure bred associate must remain our secret. We'll have to inform Lady Juliet of our intentions, of course. She doesn't like Gregson ever since he declared her demise collateral damage in an assassination plot on her idiot husband."

Watson grinned, "He never could accept the fact that she was the actual target even after Selma Fairfax was taken in, tried and hanged. He's not as thick as Athelney Jones but he doesn't like to be proven wrong."

Holmes replied, "No one is as thick as Athelney Jones. In fact Tobias Gregson is one of the better inspectors at the Yard. It's a shame Lestrade hasn't been involved in these crimes."

"Well, we'll have to deal with what we have. Shall we wait for the Baroness to return before we venture forth?"

"Where are we venturing, Gentlemen?" A sparkling contralto voice accompanied by a peremptory bark announced the reappearance of Lady Juliet and Pookie. The Baroness had changed her gown in the interim, still glistening scarlet of course, and wonder of wonders, the dog's halo was sitting at an acceptable angle. Pookie had managed to finesse her red bow, however.

"Ah, you're both back, Milady. Were you successful in getting permission to become tangible apparitions on demand?"

"Only within the confines of this assignment, Doctor. I had a little trouble convincing the Committee to include Pookie but they finally gave in. Now, what's our agenda?"

Holmes replied, *"Our first stop is Scotland Yard where we are going to offer services to track and defeat the League of the Enlightened."*

"I hope we will not have to deal with that imbecile Jones. His behavior with the Salvation Army case was unforgiveable."

"We will be approaching Inspector Gregson."

"Not much of an improvement. Mister Collateral Damage. Oh well, needs must. Shall we go? The dog and I will flit over there. I hate these London cabs."

"Wait till Watson and I organize our journey and then we'll meet you there. I assume you know where you're going."

"Oh yes, I'm most familiar with the corridors of London Law. So is Pookie. By the way, she doesn't like Gregson either and she detests Athelney Jones."

*****

50

"Sherlock Holmes and Doctor Watson. To what do I owe the pleasure of your company?"

"Pookie and I are here too, Inspector Collateral."

The dog momentarily solidified, bit Gregson's ankle and returned to her invisible state.

"Ouch!"

"Pookie, bad girl. No more of that! Although he deserved it."

Holmes and Watson, who were aware of what the Bichon had just done, struggled to control their laughter. "Are you quite all right, Inspector?"

"No, I'm not quite all right. Something just bit me."

"Has the Yard been afflicted with aggressive mice?"

"Very funny, Mr. Holmes. Sergeant, get the porters. Something bit my leg. It better not be a rat. Find it. Meanwhile, we're moving to a different room."

A short procession left and relocated in a nearby space.

Rubbing his ankle, Inspector Gregson looked at the Detective and asked, "What can I do for you gentlemen?"

Holmes replied, "It's what we can do for you. Unless you are keeping your activities secret, you seem to have terminated your pursuit of the League of the Enlightened once you had the alleged three murderers in custody."

"The League of the Enlightened is a figment concocted by those villains to take the edge off their crimes. There is no such thing."

"Allow me to disagree, Inspector. I have significant evidence to the contrary. It does exist."

Juliet sniffed, unheard *"Straight from the celestial throne room, Inspector dear."*

Holmes continued, "The Doctor and I would like the opportunity to speak with these three and hear their story."

"As would Pookie and I."

"If you want to waste your time listening to felonious fairy tales, go ahead. They are all in Newgate. Their names are Simon Clive, accused of murdering Lord Chelmsford; Archie Evans being held for the killing of Bishop Walter Mallory and Louis Stanton, felonious assault leading to the death of Brigadier George Maxwell. Stanton is also a thief."

Watson remarked, "All of their victims seem to be members of the Great and the Good. Almost sounds like assassinations. Hard to believe the deaths were all coincidences. When did these murders occur?"

"Within the past six months. Clive, Evans and Stanton have all confessed and are awaiting trial and sentencing. Probably a visit to the hangman. As far as we can tell, they don't know each other and they are being kept separate at the gaol to avoid collusion. Although I'm not sure what they would collude about."

Holmes queried, "And yet, they all tell the same story about spectral direction to kill their victims. Were their modi operandi the same?"

"No, Lord Chelmsford was garroted. The Bishop was stabbed and the Brigadier was shot."

"Curiouser and curiouser! Unless you believe their stories of being directed by supernatural beings."

Gregson snorted, "Feel free to check, Mr. Holmes. I think it's a trumped up hoax. They may have compared notes before they were arrested."

"How did you track them down?"

"Separately. They left an amazing number of clues at their crime scenes. They were incompetent amateurs."

"Or perhaps someone else left the clues to ensure they were caught."

"Anyway, they have confessed. As far as I'm concerned the cases are closed. It's up to the courts to deal with them. But to satisfy your curiosity, I'll wire the Chief Warder at Newgate and get you access to the prisoners. If you find anything significant, which I doubt, let me know."

The Baroness had remained quiet during this dialogue. *"If you want, Holmes, Pookie and I can go to Newgate and see what we can uncover before the prison bureaucracy spins its wheels and grants you and the Doctor admission."*

"An excellent idea, Milady," he replied telepathically. *"However, you will, no doubt, be horrified by the subhuman conditions there. It will be difficult to distinguish the gaolers from the prisoners."*

Holmes turned to Gregson. "Thank you, Inspector. Even though you have the prisoners in hand, I believe there is much more to these episodes than you think. These are not random killings. Some mastermind is pulling strings and is using the super or preternatural to spin his or her webs. I'll await to hear from the Chief Warder. Alacrity would be appreciated."

They rose to leave and Pookie made another pass at Gregson's ankle. This time the Baroness grabbed her before she could manifest her teeth and bite him. *"Naughty girl!"*

*****

Back at Baker Street, Holmes and Watson were descending from a cab and faced Lady Juliet and the dog sitting on the steps in front of the door. Pookie had rolled up into a ball and was snoozing. *"We realized we didn't know who we were looking for at Newgate so we decided to wait for you and the Doctor. I don't suppose you heard from the prison yet."*

"No! Join us. We need to strategize."

They went up the stairs with Juliet and Pookie floating to the top and through the door. Holmes and Watson used the more conventional mode – they climbed on foot. Watson laughed. "There are times, Holmes, when I envy them their means of propulsion. Especially when my wound is acting up."

"Just remember that in order to flit as they do, you have to be dead."

"Well, yes, there is that. Now, it seems they're able to change from ephemeral to physical at will. I almost choked when the dog bit Gregson and promptly disappeared again."

"I'm hoping they can put that ability to good use in our pursuit of the culprits. I wonder how our villains will react when faced with the real thing. We need to get a description of this woman seer from the prisoners. She may be able to lead us to this so-called Master."

They reached the sitting room door and entered to find the Baroness reading the newspaper.

"Hello, you two. I haven't been able to handle a newspaper since I died. I used to love reading my theatrical reviews or at least most of them. There are a couple of critics I'd like to haunt. This ability to go corporeal once again is refreshing. It's a shame it's only temporary. I think Pookie would like to get her teeth around a real bone."

Watson looked at her. *"How are you doing that, Milady? You and the dog seem to be able to switch states in an instant."*

"We can. On and Off. Here's Off. Watch!"

She seemed the same but the newspaper dropped. *"Oh, I forgot. You two can see me in either condition. Shall we try it on Mrs. Hudson?"*

"Good heavens, No! You'll frighten the poor woman to death."

As if on cue, the landlady tapped on the door. Watson opened it and was presented with a telegram. "A wire for you, Mr. Holmes. I think it's from Scotland Yard."

"Thank you, Mrs. Hudson. *I think Inspector Gregson has come through.*"

The Baroness huffed. *"Well, at least he's good for something."*

He read, *"Watson and I are to appear at Newgate tomorrow morning at ten. We will meet each one of the prisoners separately. Of course, you and Pookie will be our partners. It will not be pretty."*

"Thank you. In the meantime, Pookie and I shall go to the theatre and see one of the new productions. Perhaps one of those nasty drama critics will be there. Maybe I can scare him to death.

55

Although, then he'd be deceased like me. Hmm! But we'd never meet, would we? I'm sure he'd be on his way to Hell. Ta-ta! See you in the morning. I may also stop at the fashion houses and check on the latest styles. I can bring the designs back to Madame Clarice of Miraculous Modes. They love creating my outlandish gowns. C'mon girl. Perhaps we can find a real bone for you to chew on."

*****

At 30 minutes past eight the next morning, two wraiths appeared in the sitting room of 221B. Holmes and Watson were just finishing breakfast. Pookie looked longingly at a sausage on the Doctor's plate. Watson tried to ignore her but the dog won out. She materialized, snatched the extended treat and hid under the sofa with her prize.

Juliet laughed, *"You are a caution, Miss Pookie. You're lucky I'm not going to tattle on you to the Committee when we get back. You'll be a big fat slug if you're not careful. Good morning, Gentlemen. The new London theatrical season is nothing to get excited about. The Heavenly Theatre Guild's Saintly Spectaculars are far more entertaining. Perhaps that's because I'm one of their stars. Yum! That coffee smells divine. I think I might stay corporeal for few moments more and indulge. I'm going to need fortification if what I hear about Newgate Prison is true."*

*****

Newgate Prison is hardly new. Built in 1188 at the site of a gate in the Roman London Wall, the prison was extended and rebuilt many times, and has remained in use for over 700 years. There are rumors that it will soon be torn down. It deserves to be.

During most of its life, criminal courtrooms have been attached to the prison, commonly referred to as the "Old Bailey". In the late 1700s, executions by hanging took place on the public street

56

in front of the prison, drawing huge crowds and often resulting in injuries and even deaths among the spectators.

From 1868, public executions were discontinued and hangings were carried out on gallows inside Newgate. Dead Man's Walk is a long stone-flagged passageway, partly open to the sky and roofed with iron mesh. Executed criminals are buried beneath its flagstones and their initials engraved into the stone wall above. To date – publicly or otherwise – over 1100 people have been executed at the prison.

This is the fate the three felons faced for their murders. Holmes, Watson and Juliet *(plus one furry associate)* hoped to capture the criminals who induced their murderous activities. But first they needed to identify them and prove their complicity. That was the mission that morning.

The two ghosts arrived at Dead Man's Walk. Lady Juliet shivered. *"Ooh, this gaol is horrible. Pookie! What are nice girls like us doing in a place like this?"* The dog whined.

Everything they had heard about Newgate was true and then some. In spite of efforts at improvement by reformers and charitable organizations, the environment was atrocious, the prisoners miserable and the gaolers cruel, negligent or both. If you had money, you could soften your fate by buying small comforts at avaricious prices. Clive, Evans and Stanton had some resources but their condition was woeful, nonetheless.

The Chief Warder greeted Holmes and Watson, not knowing they were accompanied by two spirits. "Mr. 'Olmes! Doctor Watson. Welcome to Newgate. I 'ave pulled out your villains for you as h'inspector Gregson asked. Don't know what you'll get from them but that's yer business. Please follow me."

First on the list of villains to be interviewed was Simon Clive, accused of murdering Lord Chelmsford by garroting. They entered his cell. "Ere, Clive! You have guests. They have questions they want to ask you. None of your cheeky backtalk. I'll have a jailer with you gentlemen in case Sinister Simon acts up."

The last thing Simon Clive looked was sinister. A more miserable individual was hard to imagine. Soulless Simon was a more appropriate name. He stared vacantly and wordlessly at Holmes and Watson and of course, was unaware of Pookie and the Baroness.

Holmes addressed him. "Mr. Clive, I understand you are a banker."

A positive nod.

"We realize that you have confessed to the murder of Lord Chelmsford. Did you know him?"

A negative head shake.

The jailer barked, "Speak up, Clive. Let the gentlemen hear you!"

"No. I didn't know him."

His voice was surprisingly cultured. Clearly what you'd call a 'toff.'

"And yet you admit to killing him. Was it robbery, a bar brawl, a woman, an impulse?"

"I was commanded by the spirits."

"I'm sorry. I didn't understand that."

"No, you wouldn't. You are an unbeliever. Like Lord Chelmsford. The sprits were angry with him. He had to die. I was their agent."

"The spirits commanded you to garrote his Lordship?"

"No, the method was my choice. They simply told me he was a dangerous unbeliever and must be disposed of. I followed their instructions."

"How did you receive their instructions?"

"Through Madame. She is their intermediary."

"Who is this Madame?"

"She conducts séances for the League of the Enlightened. I don't know her real name or whereabouts. She serves the spirits."

"Where and when do these séances take place? How can I contact her?"

"You can't. She will contact you if she wishes. She conducts her séances in different places and times as it suits her, the Master and the spirits. We met at the Langham. "

"The Master? Who is he?"

"I don't know. I heard Madame speak about him. Never met him."

"Who are these spirits who commanded you to kill Lord Chelmsford?"

"They are the Avengers. Chelmsford was evil incarnate. An oppressor of the poor and destitute. They decreed he must be eliminated. I was chosen to rid the world of this scourge."

Watson spoke up. "Lord Chelmsford was nothing of the kind. He was a fighter for the working man. There are schools, orphanages and even hospitals he helped to fund. He was the leader of the British Society for Aiding the Impoverished. A great man."

Simon Clive sneered, "That's what he wanted the world to think. The spirits knew better. He was malevolent. He deserved to die. He is now rotting in Hell and I put him there."

"Do you feel any guilt for your actions?"

"No, why should I? I was doing the spirits' bidding. It was a noble act."

"Tell us about these seances."

"As I said, they took place at a suite at the Langham."

"*A luxurious locale, Holmes. I have attended a number of 'do's' there.*"

"*Yes, Baroness. I've been there too as have several of my clients. Clearly, some money changed hands here. Obviously, the League of the Enlightened is not without resources.*"

59

Watson added, *"They probably charge a great deal for their 'murder for hire' services."*

Holmes turned to Clive and said, "Go on. How did you end up in these spiritist sittings?"

"I have long been an active believer in the paranormal. I saw in the newspaper that the League was holding public séances at the Langham and I decided to attend. It is actually a social event. Drinks and canapes before the actual sessions. They charge a few pounds admission."

"And did you actively participate in the séance?"

"Not the first time."

"There were several gatherings?"

"Yes! My curiosity was aroused and I returned for another session. That time I became engaged and sought to communicate with the spirits. I was partially successful."

"Explain!"

"Several voices called my name but that was the extent of it. Then, at the end, as I was about to leave, Madame took my arm and invited me to come back for a single meeting. I was enthralled. She is quite attractive in a mysterious way."

Juliet chuckled, *"I'll bet!"*

"The private séance was held at rooms at the Savoy."

Juliet reacted. *"Ooh, pricey!"*

"When I entered, I was greeted by a server with canapes and nibbles and glasses of a strange liquor. Tart but stimulating. Madame finally arrived and we proceeded. She was a women of mystery. Dressed in black with long ebony hair. The room was darkened and we sat at a small undecorated table. That's when the spirits revealed themselves and after sharing some of their otherworld secrets, they told me I had been chosen for a special mission. They described Lord Chelmsford for the rotter that he was and told me I had been designated by the Council of Avengers to send him to his doom."

"You believed this? No hesitation or qualms of conscience?"

"Of course I believed. They were spirits in command. Who was I to doubt them? I was given his address here in London and told to dispose of him."

"How did you get the address?"

"I don't remember. Perhaps Madame gave it to me."

"Did the Avengers tell you how to go about doing Lord Chelmsford in?"

"No. I told you. That was my choice. I had just read a story in the newspaper about a man being strangled. I had no lethal weapons in my possession but it was easy to get a strong cord from my lumber room. His valet had a half day off and the rest of the staff were below stairs. I sneaked in through the garden entrance, found him asleep in his chair and strangled him. One of the footmen happened by, saw me and we struggled. He subdued me and called the constables. And here I am."

"Did you have any further contact with Madame or the spirits?"

"I hear from the spirits occasionally but nothing from Madame."

"When is your trial?"

"In two weeks. I will no doubt be hanged but it was for a good cause."

*****

We left his cell and waited for the gaoler to take us to the next prisoner. Archie Evans was being held for the murder of Bishop Walter Mallory. Evans was a somewhat different story. He hated religion in general, the Church of England and Bishop Mallory in particular. His mother had committed suicide and had been forbidden burial in sacred ground by the Bishop. Evans had seen the newspaper advert and went to the League's public séance

61

in the hope of communicating with his adored mother. He established contact but only briefly.

He was delighted when Madame took him aside and proposed a single session, this time at the Ritz. His experience was similar to Simon Clive's. A small, darkened room; preliminary snacks and drinks served by a footman; the arrival of Madame; brief discussion of the afterlife and the indignity that the Bishop had imposed on his mother. Then the Avenging Spirits took over. They urged and then instructed Evans to seek retribution from the Bishop.

At a Sunday service, Evans raced to the altar, jumped the communion rail and repeatedly stabbed the Bishop in front of a horrified congregation. He was overpowered by two deacons and taken into custody. The number of witnesses against him made it impossible for him to deny his actions. In fact, he was proud of it. The crime against his mother had been redressed.

The Baroness, in her incorporeal state, telepathically commented to Watson and Holmes. *"I have since seen Lord Chelmsford in Heaven. You were right, Doctor. His was a noble soul. I haven't come across the Bishop, however."*

Holmes chuckled, *"I doubt if you will Milady."* No further comment.

"Tell me, Evans. Was there anything unusual about the appetizers and beverages you were served at the séance?"

"Quite posh and different. I had never before tried the cocktail they served. It had an unusual taste. So did the sandwiches. I supposed they were something cooked up in the Ritz' bar and kitchens."

"Perhaps, perhaps. Well, I hope the court is lenient with you."

"I doubt it but I don't care. The Avenging Spirits and my mother are pleased and so am I."

*****

We moved on to the third cell. The smell and general atmosphere was almost unbearable. Pookie kept sneezing and sat down outside in the hallway. I told her to discorporate. Holmes said, *"Louis Stanton, charged with felonious assault leading to the death of Brigadier George Maxwell. Unlike the nobleman and bishop, the Brigadier was shot. Stanton is known as a professional thief."*

The gaoler rapped on the cell door and shouted, "Here now, Stanton. You have visitors. Be on your best behavior." He followed this with a cackling laugh.

Stanton was a different story. He had received an anonymous invitation to attend a private séance which "would be to his advantage." Hardly a believer in the afterlife or ghosts, his curiosity overcame his doubts and he appeared at the appointed time at Claridge's Hotel. He too, was wined and dined with exotic dishes and liquors by a mysterious footman who then disappeared with the arrival of Madame.

After a brief introduction to the occult which Stanton didn't credit for an instant, she began a session that brought forth minions of the underworld. The spirits he encountered supposedly came from Hell and they instructed him to recover a golden idol sacred to a tribe who worshipped the Devil. On one of his sorties the then Colonel Maxwell had taken the object from a shrine after slaughtering the natives in reprisal for their attack on his unit. For years, the statue sat in a cabinet in the now Brigadier's residence along with other spoils of war he had accumulated.

The spirits told him of Satan's desire to have his effigy returned to the tribe to reestablish their worship of him. They spoke about Brigadier Maxwell's carnage and theft of the idol. Stanton was to be the instrument of retribution. He must recover the golden statue but he could also take whatever else suited his fancy. They gave him directions and times when the house would be empty.

Although he was both dubious and amazed at the apparitions, Stanton's greed took precedence. He saw the opportunity to use the spirits' instructions and assistance to add to his own personal wealth. Rather than return the idol to the natives awaiting it in London, he would take it and other valuables he could swipe and sell them off to black market dealers he often engaged. A windfall.

Only it didn't work out that way. The night he stealthily entered the victim's apartment, the Brigadier had been taken with a case of the flu and was lying abed. Both the retired officer and his valet heard a crash when Stanton attempted to open the cabinet holding the idol. The soldier seized his service revolver which he kept under his pillow and with his valet, ran out and challenged the thief. A struggle arose and the colonel, weakened as he was, lost control of the gun. Stanton picked it up and in the melee with the Brigadier and the valet, it went off. Brigadier Maxwell fell mortally wounded. The valet wrenched the weapon away from the thief and shot him in the knee. He summoned he police and Stanton was arrested and carted away in a guarded ambulance. Maxwell was dead.

Holmes asked, "Tell me Mr. Stanton, are you recovering from your wound?"

The thief laughed, "Just in time to be hung."

"What did you make of the spirits you encountered?"

"They seemed real enough. Never believed any of that mumbo-jumbo before but they were pretty convincing."

"What about this so-called Madame?"

"Oh, she was real. Slinky sort. Tall and slim. Dressed all in black. Dark hair. Rather scary!"

"Do you remember the footman who served you?"

"Who remembers footmen? Dressed in livery. Trays on the sideboard. Cleanshaven, tall. That's all I can recall."

The gaoler, who was getting impatient, asked. "Is that all you need, Mr.'Olmes? I 'ave other duties to perform."

Holmes looked at Watson and the evanescent Baroness. They nodded. "I think we're finished here. Thank you. Good luck, Mr. Stanton!"

64

"Thanks! I'll need it. I wish I had a gold idol I could interest you in. I could have used it to pay for a solicitor."

*****

Outside the walls of Newgate, the quartet regrouped. Both the Baroness and Pookie remained incorporeal. Holmes suggested they all retire to Baker Street and review the bidding, as it were. They also needed to decide how to involve Inspector Gregson, if at all. The Detective and Doctor took a cab and the two wraiths flitted back to 221B.

Once inside the rooms, Pookie solidified, scratched her ear and barked. Mrs. Hudson was walking up the stairs and heard the dog. She opened the door to the rooms and stood staring at the little white Bichon. "How did you get in here? Who are you?" The dog disappeared. "Where did you go? I don't allow dogs in here. Come out immediately!"

Hearing footfalls, she rushed to the door. "Mr. Holmes, Doctor Watson. There's a dog in here. You know how I feel about animals in the house. I know you brought that hound Toby here once or twice and I didn't like it at all."

Holmes chuckled, "Ah Watson! The jig is up. We must face the inevitable. Prepare yourself in case she faints."

"Mrs. Hudson, let me introduce you to Lady Juliet Armstrong, the late Baroness Crestwell and her canine companion, Pookie, also deceased. They are ghosts."

"Baroness and Pookie, please show yourselves to our landlady."

The two spirits appeared. Mrs. Hudson gurgled, attempted to speak, rolled her eyes and promptly fainted. Watson rushed to her, smelling salts in hand, as he and Holmes guided her unconscious body to the chesterfield. Lady Juliet chafed her wrists but then thought better of it. She'd probably just frighten her again. The dog whined.

The landlady came around slowly. She stared trembling at the two specters and then at Holmes and Watson. Lady Juliet gave a half curtsey and said. "Sorry if we frightened you. It's the last thing Pookie and I wished to do. Holmes, I guess we'd better enlighten Mrs. Hudson."

The Great Detective proceeded to tell the history of the Baroness and Pookie. As he finished, the landlady interrupted. "I remember you. Jolly Juliet at the Palladium. A lovely voice and a wonderful comedy act. It's a shame you were shot."

"Oh, being dead has some advantages. Pookie and I are physical at the moment but we are normally ephemeral. No dangers! We can flit about, appear and disappear. We are both expert aerobatic fliers. We can spy and observe unnoticed which is what we are doing in this current case. As Holmes told you, we are on the trail of a group calling themselves the League of the Enlightened. They have been inducing subjects to commit murder and theft by claiming to be in touch with saints and demonic spirits. We intend to put a stop to that."

"My goodness, that sounds exciting. Are you the only ghosts doing detective work? I may have to change my opinion about your dog."

"We are exclusive partners with Mr. Holmes and the good doctor. I don't know of any other heavenly investigators. There may be some but I doubt it. Pookie is a very extraordinary canine. Intelligent, daring, an amazing flier, a great sense of humor and courageous. She's a wonderful companion. All the angels love her. She has terrible fashion sense, however. She is constantly tearing up her red bow and she cannot keep her halo straight. She hates baths and loves Heavenly Chewies."

On cue, the Bichon put her paws on Mrs. Hudson's lap, wagged her tail, stuck out her tongue, panted and gave her a soulful doggy look. The landlady patted Pookie's head and laughed. "She's also quite an actress. Have you been giving her drama lessons?"

"No! That seems to come naturally. I hadn't thought of it but we could probably put on a wonderful Saintly Spectacular stage routine at The Heavenly Theatre Guild. She'd probably insist on top billing."

"Holmes smiled and said, "Ladies, may we turn our attention back to the issue at hand. You may stay or leave as you see fit, Mrs. Hudson."

"Oh, I'd like to stay, Mr. Holmes. This is all very fascinating."

Watson had been taking all this in with a grin. He reached down and chucked Pookie under the chin. "Where's a good girl?"

The dog barked but stayed with her paws on Mrs. Hudson's lap. The landlady was getting the full treatment.

The corporeal Baroness looked at Holmes and Watson. "Those three all believed they were being instructed by spirits. We all know that no such thing was possible. In fact, that's why I was sent down here. To help you uncover the fraud being perpetrated by the League. They made dupes out of two fanatics and a misguided thief. But they truly believed they saw and heard commanding lifeforms. During my years on stage, I've seen some pretty clever spiritualist acts but this one sounds different. Any theories?"

"Yes," said Holmes. "Peyote!"

"She giggled. "Did you sneeze? God bless you!"

Watson struck his forehead, "Of course! They were fed a hallucinogenic before the séance. That's what the drinks and snacks were all about."

"What are you two talking about?"

"Peyote or mescaline is a psychedelic drug extracted from Mexican and South American cactus. It has been known for centuries to create a mind altering state and hallucinations. It is commonly used in native religious ceremonies to summon the gods. In this case, it induced the subjects to believe they were communicating with spirits and to obey their commands. The aftereffects lasted for several days – long enough to provoke the murderous impulses of Clive and Evans and Stanton's attempted thievery."

The Baroness squinched up her eyes. "Let me see if I understand this. The League clandestinely hires itself out as an agent for bespoke unlawful activities - often murder. Their client, probably unidentified, pays partially in advance and partially upon completion. The League then sets up and advertises a séance, Tarot reading or other spiritist event and searches among the attendees for a likely criminal candidate – usually a true believer in the occult. Sometimes it may take several events before they find a suitable dupe. When they do, they arrange a repeat one-on-one session. Priming the pump with a substantial dosage of this peyote stuff, they convince the dupe that he (or she, it could be a female) has been chosen by the spirits, gods or demons to wreak destruction on their target. Some clever theatrical effects are involved. The dupe buys in and invariably gets caught. The League disappears after being paid off by their client. We also have to determine who these clients are. How am I doing here?"

Watson laughed, "Splendidly, Milady. You should write detective stories."

"Oh, I wouldn't want to compete with you, Doctor."

Mrs. Hudson shook her head, "Incredible. It seems needlessly complicated."

Holmes smiled, "No, they are covering themselves and their client and leaving the fall guy out to dry, so to speak. To say nothing of the poor victim. They pay the dupe nothing and let him/her hang for murder. Their total expense is for the venue and the drugs."

Juliet said, "That's quite a story I'll have to tell when I return to the Elysian Fields. But we have work ahead of us. First: Who are the members of the League? Who is Madame and what about this so-called Master? Who are their clients? How do we identify them?

Second: How do we infiltrate the League, stop them and bring them to justice? Third: What do we tell Gregson and how do we get the Yard involved?"

"Are you up for an adventure, Baroness?" said Holmes.

"Need you ask, Sherlock?"

"We need someone who is immune to the effects of mescaline."

"That could be someone who is dead, I suppose."

"Someone who can communicate with the spirit world!"

"Or is a member of the spirit world."

"Someone who is an accomplished actor or actress.

"In other words, me."

"You are a perfect candidate. First, in deep disguise as an enthusiastic believer. Then as your ghostly self in the form of a commanding spirit. Pookie can be your familiar when you appear in otherworldly state. Mrs. Hudson, would you want to participate?"

"I was wondering when you were going to ask me, Mr. Holmes."

"Good. Let us keep our eyes and ears peeled for an advert from the League of the Enlightened. We can plan further then."

*****

Several days passed. Lady Juliet and Pookie got better acquainted with Mrs. Hudson, attended the theatre in ethereal form and copied off the latest fashions for Madame Clarice of Miraculous Modes back in Heaven. Finally, a small commercial notice appeared in the society pages of The Daily Express announcing a series of séances at the Grosvenor Hotel sponsored by the League of the Enlightened. Time for action!

At the appointed date and time, a stately woman, dressed in tweeds, enquired at the front desk of the Grosvenor for The League of the Enlightened. Mrs. Hudson, for it was she, was directed to a small ballroom located on the second floor where she was greeted by a young man seated at a table.

"Good morning, Madam. Welcome to the League of the Enlightened. We are always happy to welcome another true believer which I assume you are."

"Oh yes! I want to contact my late husband. (pause) The swine left me practically penniless even though he had a pile stashed away. I want to know where it is. Like most marriages. It's the woman who suffers. With all due respect, young man, I have a grievance with all men. I hear your sessions are conducted by a woman."

"Indeed! Madame is a gifted practitioner of the Occult. She has had remarkable success in communicating with the deceased spirits as well the gods and demonic entities."

"Demonic entities, eh? That sound very interesting. I look forward to meeting this woman."

The young man cleared his throat. "There is a small one pound fee to cover the cost of this venue and some refreshments that we provide to our supplicants."

(Note to Reader: One British Pound in 1900 is worth over One Hundred Twenty today. No small amount.)

"Oh well! If she succeeds in tracking Hubert down, it will be worth it." She reached into her substantial bag, pulled out a stack of notes and handed one over to the League Representative. He, in turn, handed her a descriptive brochure and welcomed her into the dimly lit ballroom. A large table covered in black velvet stood amid an array of chairs. Five black candles in the shape of a pentagram glowed alone on its otherwise bare surface. No crystal ball, decks of card or any other mystical paraphernalia. A collection of sandwiches, tea, coffee and unidentified beverages sat on a sideboard. Several men and women wandered about the room waiting for the session to begin. None of them spoke to each other.

A telepathic voice from an invisible source whispered in Mrs. Hudson's ear. *"Well, so far so good, Martha. Pookie and I are going to keep watch over this receptionist and Madame when she arrives. Keep up the misandric act. We need to convince them that you are an angry woman with a complaint against all men. Perhaps a potential killer. A poisoner!"*

Mrs. Hudson nodded. Unsure of whether the refreshments were laced with mescaline, she avoided the sideboard and took a seat next to another woman. "Good morning. I'm Martha Watson. This is my first séance."

The woman looked somewhat askance at her and then said, "You are in for a treat. This Madame is quite remarkable."

Martha replied, "It says in the brochure that she comes from the mountains of Transylvania. Is that a mystical region?"

"Oh yes, It is the center of the Occult in Europe. Wait till you see her."

"Are you a member of this League of the Enlightened?"

"No, I have not been invited to join. Only certain people are found worthy. Unfortunately, I don't seem to be one of them."

The doors to the ballroom were closed and everyone was invited to take a seat around the pentagram at the table facing a large unoccupied chair. There were six supplicants in all. Four women, two men.

Lady Juliet whispered in Mrs. Hudson's ear. *"Here she comes. She was engaged in a brief conversation with the*

71

receptionist in the hallway. He mentioned you by name and description. See if she singles you out. Then give her the 'I hate men' routine. Pookie and I will be standing by."

Soft mysterious music. From behind a dark heavy curtain, a female figure emerged and half strode, half floated to the table and unoccupied chair. A soft breeze caused the candles to flutter. Dressed in black flowing robes with a turban on her ebony tresses, she stared around the table flashing shadowy eyes lined with kohl. Around her neck hung a gold amulet. She sat with a flourish and asked the participants to join hands.

The Baroness chuckled. *"Always make a conspicuous entrance. Acting School 101."*

The Medium spoke with a well attenuated voice. "Good morning! Welcome to the League of the Enlightened. I am known simply as Madame. I am pleased and humbled that you have seen fit to join us. I feel the spirits are active today. I hope I may be of service to many of you. Please relax, empty your minds of all cares and distractions and concentrate on accepting the presence of the spirits. They are eager to communicate with you."

She gestured to the table. "A word about the Pentagram and its place in necromancy. The Pentagram expresses the mind's domination over the elements and it is by this sign that we bind the demons of the air, the spirits of fire, the specters of water, and the ghosts of earth. You may be aware of the Hermetic Order of the Golden Dawn and its magic. I apply their principles and techniques. Now, let us attempt to contact the gods, demons and spirits."

Juliet whispered. *"This is one spirit she's not going to contact today. This link to the Golden Dawn is new and probably fictitious. These villains are using it as a cover for their criminal activities. Martha, let's see if you can convince her you're worth singling out for a follow-up session. Then we'll play"*

72

The Medium stared off into space and then threw her head back in seeming ecstasy. A disembodied male voice boomed. "Who comes to seek guidance and direction."

"Aha, he's a ventriloquist," said the Baroness. *"Not bad. Probably in the theater at one time."*

Madame remained silent and motionless for a brief period and then turned toward her audience. "Our guide is here. Who wants to address him first?"

A man who wished to be reunited with his brother John spoke up. A dialogue followed in which a male voice purporting to be John reassured his brother that all was well and he was indeed happy in the world beyond. A succession of similar conversations with male and female voices took up the next half hour.

Juliet remarked telepathically, *"He's a trained ventriloquist and vocalist. He does males and females with equal skill and ease. I'm impressed. They're all done except for you. Last one up, Martha!"*

Madame looked around the room. "Is there anyone else seeking to speak with the spirits?"

Mrs. Hudson put on her most irate and formidable voice. "Yes, I want to speak with my no-good ex-husband. Where are you, Hubert? What did you do with the money? You left me penniless and deserted. Like all men, you swine. When you weren't trying to beat me you were stepping out with some floozy. I'll bet she got the blunt. I tried to be good wife but you betrayed me. I should have killed you when I had the chance. That runaway cab did it for me. I would have done you in slowly, you wretch. Just like all men, you rotter."

Silence permeated the room. The Baroness giggled. *"Well done, Martha. A performance worthy of The Heavenly Theatre*

Guild. Brava, Brava! Delay your departure. Let's see if they fall for it."

Madame looked at Mrs. Hudson. "It seems Hubert is not available. I think that concludes our séance. Thank you all for coming." She swept out of the room.

The audience stirred. Two of the women stared at Martha, whispering behind their hands. The two men walked out shaking their heads. The receptionist who had been seated near the door raised the room lights and extinguished the candles. Then he approached Mrs. Hudson.

Juliet whispered, *"Here he comes, Martha. Play hard to get!"*

"Excuse me! Mrs. Hudson, is it?" Martha nodded. "I'm sorry we were unable to establish contact with your ex-husband."

"I'm not surprised. He always was a sniveling coward. Like most men I know."

"It seems clear you have been treated poorly. Would you like another opportunity to invoke the spirits on your behalf?"

"No! I made a fool of myself in front of these people. But I am so very angry."

"I would not suggest you participate in another public effort. We do have individual sessions which Madame is willing to conduct occasionally at no charge to the supplicant. Since we failed to make contact this time, I'm sure she would be willing to provide a one-on-one séance at which you could make your feelings known to the spirits. They might be able to force your Hubert to own up to his sins."

"Well, maybe, although I doubt it will do any good. He's afraid of me. I really should have killed him when I had the chance."

The man laughed. "Well, a horse did it for you. Maybe we can find you a substitute."

Martha looked at him. "I'm not sure what you mean." (But of course she did.) "All right. I'll take a chance."

"Good! Leave your address and we will contact you."

The invisible Juliet sighed, *"As the Great Detective often says: The game is afoot. Come, Pookie. We have plans to make and things to do. We'll see you back at Baker Steet, Martha."*

*****

Sherlock Holmes and Watson listened to Juliet's and Mrs. Hudson's report. "I say, Holmes. This sounds dangerous. I'll not have Mrs. Hudson exposed any further to these villains' chicanery."

The landlady demurred. "I appreciate your concern, Doctor, but these people are killers or they incite others to kill. They can't be allowed to continue. I'm willing to keep up this charade with Lady Juliet's aid."

"Pookie and I are ready to assist. But how do we prevent the mescaline from affecting Martha?"

Holmes pulled a heavy tome down from a dust covered shelf. Oddly, the book itself was clean. "I've been exploring the subject in the British Pharmacopeia and have discovered a small monograph dealing with preventive antidotes or inhibitors for hallucinogens. One drug offsets the effects for a period of several hours. Fortunately, it has other uses and is readily available at most pharmacists. It has no harmful side effects. You must take it before ingesting any food or drink laced with mescaline. Perhaps, Doctor, you can exert your physician's privileges and procure a dose or two."

Watson set off on his assignment.

75

"I assume, Mrs. Hudson, that you have not yet been approached by these miscreants."

"No. How many of them do you think there are? Who or what makes up this League?"

Holmes replied, "I believe there are only two. The Master who is also your receptionist/host/floor manager and Madame. One of them seeks out clients, negotiates the commission and handles the payments. The other arranges and conducts the séances and triggers the commitment of the crime"

The Baroness spoke up. *"Give them this. They are a talented pair. I wonder if they started out as a variety act. He is a skilled ventriloquist. She is a pretty good actress. I'll spend the next day or so in the files at the offices of several theatrical agents. Maybe I can identify them. Another question. How do we convince Gregson to treat this as more than a hoax? He believes our three killers acted on their own motivation. He's such a fool."*

Holmes laughed, " I realize you don't like Gregson, Baroness, but he is what we must deal with. As I've said before, he and Lestrade are the best of a sorry lot. Dogged but lacking subtlety or imagination. However, I think I know how to get his attention."

"It is not frequently invoked any longer but Section 4 of the Vagrancy Act of 1824 is a great catchall to tackle rogues. That includes include 'every person pretending or professing to tell fortunes, or using any subtle craft, means, or device, by palmistry or otherwise, to deceive and impose on any of his Majesty's subjects.' I think that describes the League of the Enlightened."

Mrs. Hudson sniffed, "But surely Inspector Gregson, has more serious problems on his plate."

"Not when I get finished with him."

*****

"The client is eager for us to proceed. She is insistent that no guilt or suspicion fall back on her."

"What did you tell her?"

"That our procedures are guaranteed to protect our 'benefactors.' We have the perfect nameless agent to carry out her wishes. She will be rid of her husband in short order. She paid us one half and held the other half in escrow pending completion."

"Are you sure she'll pay up?"

"She will when she knows we can identify her. An anonymous tip to the police is always possible. Get in contact with this Hudson woman before she changes her mind. I'll lay on another supply of mescaline and you arrange a different venue for our private séance."

This conversation between the two *and only* members of the League of the Enlightened – Sylvia Gordon aka Madame and Jack McSwain aka The Master - ended without them being aware of the ghosts lurking and snooping in their presence. The previous evening Juliet and Pookie invisibly searched the files of several of London's major talent agencies and uncovered these two as the likely candidates. They had developed a mystical act for the London variety theatre that enjoyed some minor success but British audiences were fickle and impatient for new experiences. Sylvia and Jack, under financial pressure, converted their show, Voices of the East, into the murderous League with little or no effort. It was paying well and would continue to do so provided they were careful.

*****

Next morning, a telegram arrived at Mrs. Hudson's door step inviting her to a unique necromantic experience with Madame that evening in which, hopefully, her former husband, Hubert, would be called to account. This time it would be held at a private club in Belgravia. The Baroness told the others of her show business agency research and her eavesdropping on the lethal pair. From her spying, Juliet confirmed that they were using mescaline. She also rehearsed Martha in her role as a betrayed misandric housewife. Mrs. Hudson took to the character in amazing, almost frightening, fashion. Pookie and Holmes were enthralled.

Doctor Watson had procured the peyote inhibitor and instructed the landlady on its safe usage. He told her to ingest the drug-laced snacks and drinks very sparingly. Of course, the so-called receptionist would be eager to have her take large amounts.

Holmes had managed to persuade Inspector Gregson to join him, arrive clandestinely at the club and take the pair into custody once he had witnessed their illegal necromantic activities. (He owed Holmes a few favors.) They would then move on to identifying their clients and charges of incitement to murder.

Evening approached and so did Martha Hudson. With Lady Juliet and Pookie invisibly at her side, she took a cab to the club in Belgravia and announced herself to the concierge. She was directed to a small room and greeted by the League's receptionist (Jack McSwain – The Master.)

"Mrs. Hudson! How nice to meet you again. Come in! Come in! Madame is eager to see you. She will be with us momentarily. Please, have some refreshments before we start.. I think you'll find that wine quite invigorating and the sandwiches are the club's specialty." (Martha had taken the mescaline inhibitor in the cab before she entered the building.)

The darkened room was laid out in similar fashion to the larger séance venue but the table, once again covered in black with candles arrayed in a pentacle, was smaller with only two chairs. McSwain engaged in small talk while urging the landlady to eat and drink.

Martha insisted on excoriating her fictional husband. "I'd like to get my hands on that swine. Hubert's like all men, present company excluded, I'm sure. Taking advantage of women and skipping off. He won't appear. He's afraid! Oooh, I'm so angry. It's almost uncontrollable." (She took a dainty swig of the wine.) "This stuff tastes peculiar. What's in it? You're not drugging me, are you?"

Juliet laughed and Pookie barked. *"Atta girl, Martha. Keep him off balance."*

The Master looked shocked. "Of course not, my dear. What a terrible thought. Ah, Madame has arrived. I shall leave you two alone. Drink up! I hope the spirits are active. We must have you satisfied."

He left (hiding in the dark at the far side of the room) and the Medium wafted into the salon. dressed as she was in the earlier session. She sat and waved at Mrs. Hudson to take the other chair. She extended her hand and touched the landlady's arm. "The spirits are with us. Finish your drink and we will proceed."

The Baroness grinned. *"Little does she know. Pookie. The spirits are indeed present and accounted for. Martha, let's allow Madame to do her act before we appear."* The dog growled and wagged her tail.

The lights in the room dimmed until only the candles provided any illumination. Once again, ominous music played in the background. (The Master was applying all the tricks of the trade.)

Madame (Sylvia Gordon) grabbed the table, threw back her head and in a moaning voice queried. "Spirits, are you with us?"

A booming voice responded. "Who calls?"

"A supplicant desires guidance and contact. Where is Hubert?"

"He is not here. He will not come."

Martha snarled and shouted, now supposedly under the influence of the mescaline. "The rotter. I knew he wouldn't show up. I want revenge."

The voice replied. "You shall have it. There is a man worse than Hubert who has been victimizing women such as yourself. His name is Arthur Moorhead. A banker. He lives here in Belgravia. You will take the poison Madame will give you and use it to send him to Hell. Do you understand?"

Martha shrieked, "I understand and I will comply. I will be avenged."

Holmes and Gregson had slipped into the darkened room in time to hear this exchange. The Inspector was about to arrest the Medium when Holmes held his arm. "Wait a moment!, he whispered.

Suddenly a little white dog appeared, growled and jumped onto Madame's lap. She screamed. Juliet appeared, flickering in her scarlet dress and said in her most theatrical contralto. *"No, Sylvia. It is you and Jack who will be sent to Hell to suffer for your crimes The spirits have ordained this."*

"What the…" McSwain rushed out from behind the curtains and grabbed at the Baroness. He came away with fists full of air. He fell on his face.

"Naughty, naughty, Master. Don't you know enough not to attack a ghost?" Juliet and Pookie disappeared. Madame fainted.

Gregson overcame his shock enough to put handcuffs on both of them and with tremulous voice read them their rights. A pair of large constables who had been outside came in and dragged them out.

The Inspector turned to Holmes and asked. "Who was that?"

"An actress friend and her pet dog. She specializes in magic acts. Appearing and disappearing. She's gone now. I think you'll find that these two were behind the three killings I asked you to investigate.. I'm sure Clive, Evans and Stanton will identify them. You need to identify their clients."

Gregson was pleased with the catch. As usual, Holmes would allow Scotland Yard to take full credit. He was dubious about Holmes explanation of Juliet and Pookie but didn't press the point.

Mrs. Hudson, relieved that the event was over and had ended well, whispered. "Well done, Lady Juliet."

A ghostly voice replied, *"You too, Martha. Bravissima!"*

A dog barked.

The Girls' night out

"I suppose you and Pookie will be heading back to your celestial mansion and incorporeal state, Baroness, now that we have dismantled the League of the Enlightened."

"Eventually, Martha, but we're in no hurry. Pookie and I are enjoying being able to materialize at will. I'm sure Mr. Raymond will have to send an Archangel after us if we tarry too long but I think we can squeeze another evening on the town out before we have to return. The Heavenly Behavioral Committee is made up of a bunch of fuddy duddies but Raymond is a sweetheart. How woud you like to join Pookie and me in a little frivolity to celebrate our victory over the Mystics of Evil?"

This conversation was taking place between Mrs. Hudson, landlady to Sherlock Holmes and Doctor Watson and Lady Juliet Armstrong, Baroness Crestwell (deceased but with her dog, Pookie, still hyperactive.)

"I'd love it but surely we should invite Mr. Holmes and the Doctor to accompany us."

"I've already done that but they are both on their way to Cornwall to look into what Mr. Holmes describes as "yet another jewel theft." He did make a very generous donation for us to enjoy dinner and a show. The dog and I no longer need money when we are our ghostly selves but if we are going to celebrate in the flesh so to speak, cash is a necessity. And of course, that applies to you."

"Well, two ladies and a dog might turn a few heads but who cares. Our last adventure has stirred up a sense of daring in me that I thought was dead."

"My death increased my sense of daring. What else could possibly go wrong?"

"You seem to be enjoying your life after death."

"Yes, in spite of all my whinging, I really do but a little more life after life isn't bad either. Now, what do you want to do? How about if we start off the afternoon by buying you a new dress, go on to a show and finish off with a posh dinner. We'll find some tasty snacks for Pookie."

"That sounds so extravagant."

"We're spending Sherlock Holmes' money. I think Doctor Watson tossed in a few quid, too."

"Well, in that case!"

*****

Two stately and classically dressed women and a little white dog emerged from Liberty and Company's emporium on Regent Street and took a cab back to 221B Baker Street. Mrs Hudson tripped up to her rooms to change for her evening on the town. Lady Juliet snapped her fingers and was instantly encased in a daring scarlet frock of Parisian design, produced by Miraculous Modes of Heaven. Pookie sported a red bow and a stylish halo that she would relinquish when they went on their evening jaunt. Some of the venues they would be visiting frowned on animals so she would have to appear and disappear as necessary. No problem. She was sure of a tasty dinner under the table at Simpson's in the Strand.

She also liked the musical theatre. Unlike most of her canine counterparts, she had a melodic ear and a keen sense of rhythm which stood her in good stead when she danced, wagged her tail in tempo or engaged in aerobatic maneuvers. Like her mistress, a true showdog. But a showdog who excelled in celestial aerial dogfights.

First stop, the Palladium, Juliet's old "stomping grounds" when she could still stomp. They took up excellent seats in the stalls and sat back to watch a timeless musical comedy – 'Where's Jane?' Mrs. Hudson was informed that during her days on the stage, Juliet Armstrong played Jane in several productions.

Oh, Oh! As the house lights dimmed and the orchestra took up the overture, a rustling sound came from the seat next to Mrs. Hudson. A woosh and a thump and Pookie was sitting on her lap. Surprisingly, she had grown quite fond of the little dog. The Baroness had flitted down to the stage where she, hopefully unseen to others, had joined the chorus as the curtain rose and they pranced across the proscenium, singing something inane about Spring, flowers, boys, girls and love. As they ended their number, a ridiculously handsome matinee idol took up center stage, looked left, looked right, stared at the audience and shouted, "I say, where's Jane?"

As the puzzled members of the chorus fussed, looked about and queried each other, the invisible *(except to Mrs. Hudson)* Lady Juliet twirled toward him, planted a kiss on his masculine cheek and flitted back to her seat in the stall next to the delighted landlady. Pookie resumed her place on the Baroness' lap.

Juliet giggled silently and telepathically said, "I hope he finds her. Blimey, Martha, that was fun. Not up to the standards of the Heavenly Theatre Guild's Saintly Spectaculars but fun, nonetheless. Oh here comes the ingenue now. Doing her entrance solo. Sad and disappointed in love. Pretty but she can't hold a note. I remember when singers had to know how to sing. She's not much of an actress, either. Probably a 'friend' of the producer."

Martha looked shocked. "Surely not!"

"Welcome to show business, Mrs. Hudson."

*****

The first act wandered its turgid way toward conclusion, the curtain fell and the house lights rose. Time for the interval. Juliet, once again solidly corporeal, rose and said, "Come Martha! I ordered some champagne from the theatre bar. We need a little fortification if we're going to last it through to the finale. This production is terrible. Pookie, stay here and I'll bring you back a bowl of champagne and some nice bar snacks. Don't forget we still have dinner ahead of us at Simpson's."

They slowly progressed up the aisle to one of the bars where two flutes of second-rate champagne awaited them. Juliet huffed, "Oh, how the Palladium has fallen. This champagne is as flat as this production. Bubbly, it's not."

Suddenly a slurred declaration rang out from behind her. "Oh, I say! Juliet Armstrong!"

The Baroness recognized the all too familiar voice and mildly shuddered. This evening's escapade was turning into a disaster. It was Reginald, Baron Crestwell, her former husband. What was he doing in London? She heard through Holmes of the appointment of Baron Reginald Crestwell as His Highness' personal representative to the court of the Maharajah of Sailendra. Wherever that was. Time to call on her acting skills. At least there would be one worthwhile performance this evening. Martha Hudson was mesmerized.

"I'm sorry, sir. Were you addressing me? I'm afraid we have not been properly introduced."

"Not introduced? You're my wife. I thought you were dead!"

Reginald reached for her but slipped. Mrs. Hudson gasped.

85

Juliet stared him down with her best aristocratic sneer. "How dare you! I am not your wife, never was and as you can see, I am very much alive. Come Martha, I have had quite enough of this show."

His jaw dropped as she strode off holding a bowl of champagne for the dog. Mrs. Hudson scurried after her.

"Who is he, Baroness?"

"I will give you Mycroft Holmes' assessment. Quote. *'Reginald, Baron Crestwell, my one time husband. A pompous twit and an infernal pest. Unfortunately, he has major connections to the Royal Household! More specifically, he and Crown Prince Bertie are carousing playmates! Crestwell has been responsible for more agency cockups than a regiment of chimpanzees.'* Unquote.

Martha asked, "What agencies?"

"Take your pick. Home Office, Foreign Office, the Army, the Admiralty, the Auditor. They pass him around like yesterday's dirty laundry. None of them has the guts to just throw him out and anger His Highness."

They reached the seats and Juliet fed the champagne to Pookie who lapped it up. She gobbled the bar snacks. The Baroness continued.

"Reginald is a stupid blowhard. I really wonder why I married him. Oh, I guess I do. I liked being a Baroness. Anyway, he was always ready to prove how important he is to anyone who'll listen. So who was listening? Selma Fairfax, that's who. She was a German spy and paid to have me killed. She was proud of it. She hired two known assassins to do the deed. He was collateral damage."

"After he recovered from his wounds, he was sent off as the Government's representative to the court of the Maharajah of Sailendra. Now he's back. The idiot probably set off a revolution."

"Are you two ready for a delicious dinner? Let's leave. This show will not get any better. Trust me. Give me a few minutes first to go to the Ladies and we can head for Simpson's. When a spirit becomes corporeal again, all of the bodily functions reactivate. Wait till we get outside, Pookie"

*****

Early next morning, Holmes and Watson returned from Cornwall. False alarm. The stolen jewels were simply misplaced by the dotty mistress of the manor. She had the good grace to pay for their expenses and a pro-rated fee.

Juliet and Pookie were preparing to shed their alternate physical makeups and return to their celestial bowers. She thanked Holmes and the Doctor profusely for financing their night out. Mrs. Hudson was all over herself in enthusiasm and gratitude, showing the detectives her new dress from Liberty, raving about the magnificent fare at Simpson's, but bemoaning the performances at the Palladium, only livened up by the Baroness' high-jinks. Then she turned to Juliet. "Tell them about meeting your ex-husband, Lady Juliet. That was a near thing."

This got Holmes and Watson's immediate attention. They both stared at the Baroness. She grinned. "Of all the gin bars in all the towns in all the world, he walks into the one I'm in. I couldn't believe it. I managed to fluff him off."

"Reginald Crestwell?"

"None other!"

Watson coughed, "The Reginald Crestwell found dead in a box at the Palladium Theatre last night?"

Juliet choked, "What? What are you talking about? I don't know what you mean."

Holmes looked at her. "Your ex-husband was done in violently during the second act of Where's Jane?. At the Palladium." He held out a copy of the Daily Mail. The headline screamed;

"Diplomat Murdered While The Show Goes On!"

A diplomatic representative of Her Majesty's Government was found strangled late last evening in a luxury box at the Palladium Theater. Baron Reginald Crestwell, a well known figure in society and international embassies had just been called back to England after a bloodless revolt overthrew the Maharajah of Sailendra to whom he had been accredited. As of yet Scotland Yard has no clues as to the assailant's identity. Members of the public with relevant information are asked to contact the police as soon as possible.

The Baroness stared at the article. "Reginald dead!? How ironic. Everyone thought he was the target when I was shot. I couldn't stand him but I shall pray for his soul. Speaking of which, I'll contact Raymond and see if he has been taken to the Pearly Gates."

There was a pause. "Oh dear, Raymond says he was not one of the candidates for entrance on this morning's Angelic Shuttle. That doesn't bode well. Pookie, you and I are being summoned back. It seems we have used up our corporeal time here on Earth. Martha, I am glad you can now see us. No doubt we will make another visit and it will be such fun to share time and gossip with you." She hugged her.

The landlady touched a lace handkerchief to her eyes. "I shall look forward to it, Milady and you too, Pookie."

"Holmes, Doctor, I'm sure we'll be seeing more of each other."

"Very probably. Baroness. Give my regards to Mister Raymond."

The ghosts disappeared.

Mrs. Hudson stared at the spot they had occupied and then turned to Holmes. "You don't suppose, do you?"

"What, Mrs. Hudson?"

"Well, last night, we decided to leave the theatre at the interval after drinking glasses of terrible champagne. We collected Pookie and then Lady Juliet said she wanted to make a stop at the Ladies. I thought it strange that a ghost would need to use the facilities but she laughed and said when she went physical, so did all of her systems. She strode off. I thought nothing further of it. The dog and I waited and she soon returned. Sure enough, Pookie had to go too and relieved herself once we got outside. Off we went to Simpson's and had a wonderful dinner. But now I wonder. Instead of using the loo, could the Baroness have flitted away and done her ex-husband in?"

Watson was horrified, "Surely not, Mrs. Hudson. The Baroness is a…saint. Heaven would never have admitted her or allowed her to stay. You can't honestly believe that…Holmes, what do you think?"

"No, Mrs. Hudson. Lady Juliet can be shocking but murderous? Never. To relieve your mind, we shall investigate and find the real killer of Baron Reginald. I doubt Scotland Yard has made much progress."

"Yes, Sherlock. Baron Crestwell's assassination is under investigation by Scotland Yard, the Home and Foreign Offices and my own staff. So far, we have little to go on beyond the unrest in Sailendra. The Maharajah and his retinue have all fled here. The Baron was called back by the Foreign Secretary."

"There is a strong rumor that he was found on the wrong side of a romance with a member of the court. He always was a bit of a bounder. His ladies have been unfortunate. First, Lady Juliet was shot. Then Selma Fairfax was arrested, tried and hung for The Baroness' murder. Now it seems there was an 'honor killing' of the young courtesan who had taken up with Reginald the Rake. Her father and brothers were probably responsible for terminating the 'infidel' but given the discordant situation in the princedom, we have no reliable way of pursuing the killers with any certainty."

Mycroft Holmes stared at the ceiling. "I suppose I will have to inform His Highness! Bertie will not be pleased."

*****

"So you see, Mrs. Hudson, the police believe Baron Crestwood was the victim of a family honor killing."

"Oh, Mr. Holmes, how horrible and barbaric. The poor girl and the poor Baron. I am so ashamed I doubted dear Lady Juliet. Do you think she could forgive me?'

"She didn't know what you thought and we have no intention of telling her. Doubts arise in all criminal situations. You just keep on being her friend and Pookie's as well.

Ah yes, Pookie. Such a sweet dog!

The Canine Cadre – a novella

As usual, the cosmic sun was gleaming in Heaven, casting a mild, comforting warmth and gentle glow, more than enough for seeing clearly but not a glare to be filtered or a burn to be avoided. Perfect sunshine in a perfect sky in a perfect place. A beautiful, dark-haired wraith surveyed the situation.

"Another splendid day here in the hereafter. Oddly enough, I find myself with nothing much to do. No classes, no sitting for Leonardo DaVinci, no theatre rehearsals, no fittings, no flying lessons. What say, Pookie? A romp on the Elysian Fields?"

Lady Juliet Armstrong, the late Baroness Crestwell, suddenly realized she was talking to herself. Clad in one of her scarlet day dresses, she looked around her otherworldly mansion. Soft music, gentle breezes, flowers galore, and the latest round of furnishings from Celestial Real Estate but…no dog! Now where had that little adventuress gone off to?

"Pookie! Pookie? Where are you?"

Suddenly she realized she was not alone. Mr. Raymond, Heaven's Senior Director, was hovering a few inches off the floor of her opulent entranceway.

"Lady Juliet! Greetings! You seem distressed. Have you lost something or someone?"

"Pookie is making herself scarce. You wouldn't know anything about that, would you?"

"Yes, in fact, I would. The dog has gone to the Meadows."

91

"The Meadows. Isn't that where the deceased animals go to relax and gambol awaiting admission to Heaven over the Rainbow Bridge. What is she doing there?"

"Meeting with some of her colleagues. Don't worry. She's fine. She hasn't been expelled from Paradise although there are times when the Committee has been tempted to."

"I guess that applies to me too."

"I couldn't possibly say, Milady. However, I came to bring you there. You've never been through the entire location and you should. Given your association with Sherlock Holmes, there's someone there I want you to meet."

"What has Sherlock Holmes got to do with the Meadows?"

"You'll find out. Now, if you'll follow me. It's just a short flit."

Like everything else celestial, the Meadows extended infinitely but took up no space at all. Juliet had only visited the expanse once when Pookie had joined her at her first arrival in Paradise. Not that she wasn't interested but her other activities had captured most of her time although in Heaven, time was limitless. They approached the Meadows by exiting the Pearly Gates, waving at St. Peter enroute and out over the Rainbow Bridge.

"Doesn't he get bored manning the entry desk?"

"Not at all! He's a master of bilocation, actually multilocation. He holds down the entry portal but spends much of his time in the Throne Rooms talking over old times on Earth with the Apostles and the Almighty. He's quite flexible. This is a multiverse after all. Look, We're coming up at the Meadows now."

The Baroness floated upward in order to get a comprehensive view of the complex. It did indeed look limitless. Long plains of sunlit grass dotted with every variant of tree, bush and botanical stretched farther than the eye, even the celestial eye, could see. A large body of water, fed by waterfalls extended far off in several directions. Was that a herd of elephants splashing and drinking? Deer, gazelles, zebras boars, pigs and, good heavens, giraffes all approached the shoreline. A sleuth of bears. *(Yes, Octavius. That's what they are called.)* She could see schools of fish and other aquatic animals hurtling over, through and under the gentle waves. An alligator basked in the sun. Wonder of wonders, beasts who were predators on earth showed no signs of hostility toward any of their fellows. This indeed was the peaceable kingdom.

A huge golden structure appeared in a low lying cloud. It turned out to be a formation of buildings surrounding a large hall. Raymond called out. "Mr. Sherman, greetings. I have someone I want you to meet."

A short, wizened gentleman accompanied by a pair of angels and two young celestials emerged from the hall's lavish entrance. A pair of puppies and a kitten cavorted at his feet.

"Mr. Raymond. You're always welcome. Who is this lovely creature?"

"I'd like you to meet Lady Juliet Armstrong, the late Baroness Crestwell. She is a good friend of Sherlock Holmes and Doctor Watson."

Juliet did a playful curtsey. Raymond continued, "Lady Juliet. This is Mr. Sherman. A relatively recent arrival in Paradise who has most generously agreed to manage the Meadows along with his angelic and heavenly partners." Please meet Charles, Lucia, Astrophel and Daria. They are part of his rotating staff. He bowed in their direction. They returned the gesture, the angels' iridescent wings fluttering in the gentle breeze.

Sherman said, "We're very pleased to meet you, Milady. You are the companion of Pookie, if I am properly informed. The little scamp is here visiting with her canine associates. I am a naturalist. Before my death, I maintained a large menagerie in my home in Lambeth. Among my charges was the famous canine detective, Toby, his mate Celeste and their pups. That is how I came to know Sherlock Holmes. He employed Toby's extraordinary stalking skills in many of his adventures. Toby and Celeste are now here at the Meadows living an afterlife of leisure with their doggie friends."

Raymond interrupted. "That is why we are here, Mr. Sherman. Mr. Holmes would like to employ Toby's formidable tracking ability which I believe he has retained even after his death. The detective has made the request of me and I am more than inclined to accommodate him after several favors he has performed for Heaven."

"I'll speak to the dog but where are my manners. Perhaps, Lady Juliet would like a tour of the Meadows and this facility before we get down to business."

"That would be lovely," she replied. "Thank you, Mr. Sherman. I am amazed at the size, scope and variety of this place. How do you manage?"

"Most of the animals self-manage. They are quite competent. Come, let me show you. He waved his hand and a glittering map floated before their eyes. You've seen the expanse of assorted undomesticated animals as well as the lakes, ponds, salt oceans and watercourses where the aquatics and semi-aquatics reside but we have a few territories set aside for individual species. The avian, primate, ovine, bovine, equine, feline and canine, to name the most populous. The dinosaurs have their own separate

94

jungle. They were here first and don't associate with mammals or other species. They believe they are the ancestors of the birds."

"So, first stop: The birds. The Meadows is one gigantic aviary. Look up all around you. The sky is full of them. From condors and eagles to canaries and budgies; starlings by the thousands; robins; bluebirds, wrens, orioles and of course, cardinals of the non-religious sort; hawks; falcons; songbirds galore; pheasants and others who no longer have to worry about being game birds. We have the flightless varieties like the emu, ostrich and cassowary; shore birds; pelicans, storks, albatross and the consummate show off – the peacock. All living together peacefully. Not a predator in the flock. Astrophel, tell them about your charges."

Astrophel was an exceptionally handsome angel. *(They all are!)* He shrugged his wings down his back and said, "I watch over the primates. Apes, monkeys, chimps! Here, let me show you."

An immense cluster of trees and bushes appeared before them. Hairy bodies of all sizes hurtling, jumping and bumping through the foliage. Chattering, grunts, thumping and groans. A symphony of uncoordinated sounds.

Juliet winced. "How do you stand all that noise?"

The angel reached at the sides of his head, laughed and said, "Cosmic earplugs!"

"Next, the sheep and goats. They are Daria's charge. She is a shepherdess angel."

That spirit fluttered her wings, a large image emerged and they beheld a vast lawn of succulent grass dotted with clusters of white, grey and an occasional spot of black. Rams, ewes and lambs! And goats! Nannies, billies and babies. Munching blissfully on tender blades that renew themselves as soon as they are eaten. Daria smiled. "The Lord stops by here every day and checks up. After all, He is The Shepherd and this is one of His flocks."

"We also have grassy spreads for cows and horses. Some of the steeds are wild but our domesticated equine guests vary from plough, cab and wagon horses to famous racers, show and circus performers. You may be familiar with one or two, Lady Juliet, from your theatre days."

"Yes, there was a performing palomino named General who was a particular favorite of mine. I rode him bareback. Him, not me. What a star! Such a lovely gentleman! I don't suppose he is here."

"No, happily, General crossed over the Rainbow Bridge to be with his trainer when she died. You'll find him closer to your home. Here, let Lucia tell you about the cats."

Lucia was a celestial on a temporary learning assignment at the Meadows. Fortunately or unfortunately, she was assigned to the felines.

She laughed, "Charles went to the dogs and I got the cats. Independent creatures, clever, temperamental, beautiful, sly. You've heard the phrase 'Like herding cats.' Try it some time. They believe they're the only ones here in the Meadows and they don't seem much concerned about crossing the Rainbow Bridge. We're lucky in one sense, however. Many of the newly arrived human denizens of heaven owned a cat or two and promptly reclaim them. Same with dogs, I imagine. Here let me show you."

She waved her hands and an image of an immense hall filled with trees and vertical structures came into view. A vast assortment of cats, domesticated and wild, jumped, pounced, strutted, ran, snoozed and sat licking their fur and paws. Siamese, calicos, tabbies, Persians, short hairs, long hairs, angoras. Several lions were asleep but three lionesses looked up. A cheetah was tussling with an ocelot. Two pumas pranced with several jaguars in a tug of war. Looking over all of this was a gigantic tiger. A beautiful snow leopard strode through the trees. Impossible to count them all.

"As you know, unlike the deceased humans, the animals here still eat. Cats are very finicky feeders. We've had to invent a special brand of Heavenly Chewy for them. Not the stuff dogs snarf. Heaven forfend! They have a recipe all their own. I've been working in the kitchens to perfect the culinary treat. I think we've finally got it. OK, Charles, time for the dogs or are you going to show them, Mr. Sherman?"

"Thanks, Lucia. Yes. Charles, I'll take it. Let me introduce you, Baroness, to my canine corps. Of all the animals we have, these are the dogs I have come to truly know and love. Come with me." Instead of making an image appear, he flitted away from the entrance hall with his staff. Juliet and Raymond followed.

Even before they arrived at their target, they were greeted by a cacophony of growls, whines, snarls, barks and howls. *(All in good fun.)* A grassy expanse that seemed to have no end was the site of a game of sorts with no apparent rules except taking and keeping possession of a by now, slobber-covered ball. The Meadows Doggie Bowl. Pookie was in the middle of it. There were several other small white dogs all expressing themselves as they dodged each other diving for the sphere. One stood to the side and barked incessantly.

Mr. Sherman laughed. "That's Marshall. Protesting the calls as usual. He also chases the morning and afternoon Angelic Post Chariots when they come by. Never catches them. There's Woof, Pookie's cousin. Both Bichons. The two of them are adventuresses. Never know what they'll get into next. That other curly white one is probably a Maltese. We're not sure. Her name is Buttons. Black eyes and nose. Sassy but affectionate! The Black and Tan Terrier is Tinker. They don't come any sweeter but he's giving the crew a real battle for the ball. See that slightly bigger white girl with the black oblong spots. That's Miz Chips, a real senior citizen as is the black and white taking a drink. That's Chubby and he really is. The brown guy who just lost the ball is Hobo. Not the brightest but really lovable. The cheerleader is Penny Lane – Miss Excitement. "

"We also have three friends from America's Wild West. Gizmo, Bailey and Cinco from far off Arizona. Cinco is bi-lingual. He barks in English and Spanish. He also does landscaping. Gizmo and Bailey are smart. Real smart."

"And now, Baroness and Mr. Raymond, the stars you really want to meet,. Toby and his mate Celeste. We were together when we were all alive in London. They protected my establishment."

"Toby didn't exactly live with me. He and his missus and their two pups had digs next door. We had an arrangement. I provided them with food and drink, and he protected my home and my animals. I was a naturalist, Lady Juliet. Still am. I had creatures there that the London Zoo would have loved to get their paws on. I was constantly fighting them off. I guess they have them now. Toby and Celeste did quite a job. I really hated to lose them when they died but now we're back together. Mr. Holmes found good residences for their two puppies. Let's go talk to them. Come along, Baroness. You know Holmes better than any of us."

They walked over to the sideline while the game was still going on. Pookie recognized the Baroness, looked a bit embarrassed but kept on fighting for the ball. Nobody was going to beat out the Heavenly Dog Fight Champion. Toby and Celeste were acting as referees. At Sherman's gesture, Toby broke off from the game, leaving his mate to manage the skirmish.

He trotted over to the naturalist and accepted a few pats on his substantial head. Imagine an ungainly, long-haired, lop-eared canine, breed indeterminate, brown and white in colour. Nothing about his appearance gave any indication of the intelligence, skill, determination and courage embedded in that nondescript body. Toby, mortal or ghost, was an original.

Sherman stared at him and the dog stared back quizzically. "Toby, I realize you and Celeste are here to rest and relax after the strenuous life you led on Earth but we have a request for your services by none other than Mr. Sherlock Holmes."

At the mention of Holmes' name, the dog tilted his head and fiercely wagged his tail. No question whether he recognized the name. His canine memory banks were active. Sherman continued, "Toby, you know Mr. Raymond. This lovely lady is Baroness Crestwell, a good friend of Mr. Holmes." The dog extended his paw to Juliet. She accepted. Pookie had dropped out of the game, moved to the sideline and was watching this activity. She jumped over and put her paws up on the Baroness' knees and stared menacingly at Toby.

Juliet laughed. "No need for jealousy, little miss. Toby has agreed to do some work for Mr. Holmes. It's him he's interested in. Not me!"

Raymond looked at her. "Would you and Pookie consider going back to Earth with Toby and Celeste. The dogs will be ghostly and will need an intermediary to act with Holmes."

The Baroness, as usual, welcomed the opportunity to interact once more with the Great Detective to say nothing of Watson and now, Martha Hudson. She and Mrs. Hudson got on swimmingly. Not wanting to seem too eager, she gave it a moment or two of thought and then said, "All right, but it's Pookie who will have to act as intermediary with Toby and Celeste. They talk dog. I can talk to Pookie. She'll need to translate for Toby and Celeste. What's the assignment, Raymond?"

"I don't know Baroness. I need someone to talk detective."

*****

Back on Earth, Sherlock Holmes turned to Doctor Watson and said, "I have had news from Mr. Raymond. He has arranged to have Toby and his mate Celeste assist us in tracking down the absent Mr. Cornhill. A case reminiscent of Mr. James Phillimore. You remember. He went back into his house for an umbrella and was never seen again."

"We will be graced by the presence of Lady Juliet and her dog Pookie. Toby and Celeste are totally ephemeral and will require intermediaries to communicate with us. Since we have no such problem with the Baroness, we can deal directly with her and she in turn with them."

Watson raised an eyebrow. "That sounds a bit complicated, Holmes. She can communicate with us but can she talk to the dogs? For that matter, if Toby is incorporeal, does he still have his famous skill of tracking. You will recall his sensitivity was all in his nose."

"The answer to your first question is yes. Lady Juliet speaks to her dog Pookie regularly and the canine understands her. I sometimes believe she even answers the Baroness. It should be the same with Toby and Celeste. To your second query. I don't know. We'll find out as soon as they arrive. We'll run a test"

As if on cue, three dogs and a scarlet clad wraith flitted into the sitting room of 221B Baker Street. Pookie ran first to Holmes and then Watson, feverishly wagging her tail. Toby sniffed around tentatively and then approached Holmes. Celeste politely held back. The Baroness gave a tinkling laugh and said, "Well Holmes, your canine cadre has arrived. Oh, and me too. Mr. Sherman sends his regards. The dogs and I have been getting acquainted. I think Pookie is a bit jealous of Toby but for all her talents, she is only a so-so tracker. We need the big fellow and his mate. Where's Martha Hudson? I do so want to see her again"

"Greetings Baroness! Delighted to have you join us. And your doggish friends. You are all most welcome. Mrs. Hudson will appear as soon as she knows you've arrived. Meanwhile, make yourself comfortable." *(They already had.)*

Juliet stared at the detective. "Now that we are here, why are we here? Raymond told us little and Sherman didn't know."

"We have a disappearance on our hands that has given me pause. Josiah Cornhill Jr., a London industrialist, has vanished without a trace. Scotland Yard and the rest of the Met are not giving it much credence. They say it's not all that unusual for an adult male to leave home and not return. His wife and family think otherwise. As does his father who is the chairman of Cornhill Enterprises Ltd. In Hammersmith. The board of directors of that company has commissioned me to find the young man. He is the Director of Production for their manufacturing facilities. They make parts for steam and petrol engines. I hope our good friend Toby here will be invaluable in finding him, preferably still alive."

Toby barked at the sound of his name. Watson grinned. "Well maybe we won't have any problem conversing with Toby and the lady Celeste, after all."

Juliet asked, "Holmes, how did you meet Toby and Celeste? If it's not too sensitive a subject, how did they die? Mr. Sherman evaded my questions. For that matter, how did he pass on?"

"As to how we met! After a particularly complicated and intense case involving smugglers, Wiggins, a highly intelligent but marginally educated leader of the ragged group of urchins, the Irregulars, whom you have met, came to me and said, "Beggin yer pardon, Mr. 'Olmes but me and the fellows *(there was also a girl, but she dressed as a boy.)* would like to make a sergestion. *(Holmes slipped into a very good version of a cockney street urchin accent.)* We think you need another member of the group. This last job was a bit of a trial and we know someone who would have made short work of the whole thing. Name's Toby. He's a dorg."

"A dog?"

"Not just any dorg, Mr. 'Olmes. He's a ruddy genius dorg. We've used him several times without your knowing it. No extra charge! A good beefy bone and he's in heaven. He's got a nose that can sniff its way to a target in a crowd of stinkin' sweaty longshoremen or a parade of perfumed tarts. But it's not just his nose. He's smart. Smarter than the average copper or thug. In fact, he made a monkey out of your friend Lestrade, just last week. Found a gun the Peelers and the Yard had been searchin' for fer weeks. You need to meet Toby."

"I agreed. I needed to meet Toby. I did and I was awestruck. The dog was indeed a genius."

"As to his death, Toby passed on like the brave and wonderful animal that he was. He was defending me."

He shook his head. "It happened in Park Lane of all places. I had received a call from Gregson to assist in what looked like a violent kidnapping or worse. You may remember from the papers, the case of Lady Chesterfield - a dowager who lived with her nephew in an opulent, multi-storey town house. She had gone missing or so the servants had reported. The nephew was out of town at the time, supposedly at a reunion in Oxford."

"Several of the rooms including the lady's bedroom were in serious disarray and according to her maid, more than a few of her most valuable pieces of jewelry were gone. She had just returned from a house party and had not yet put them away. She told the maid she was exhausted, and her services would not be required for the rest of the evening."

"About one AM, the butler thought he heard a series of noises and a scream. He got up, ran into the hall and saw the door to the lady's suite was open. There were signs of a struggle, but her ladyship was gone. The lady's maid and a footman immediately started a search while the butler summoned Scotland Yard. Very early next morning, Inspector Gregson called and asked for my assistance. Given the nature of the supposed crime, I decided to call Watson and had Wiggins bring over Toby. If there was a missing person, the dog was an expert."

"Our opening supposition was that a burglar had been surprised by Lady Chesterfield and he attacked her. But if so, was she dead? Where was the body? Toby found her under a pile of coal in the basement, shot twice."

"The nephew had returned and was suitably upset. He said he had just gotten back from Oxford. A call to the Inn where the event had taken place confirmed that he had not registered or signed in for the festivities. The inspector asked him where he had really been, and he had no satisfactory answer. He broke from the room and headed up the stairs with all of us in pursuit. He pushed a large urn down on us just missing Watson. I rushed up toward him. Toby was ahead of me. Gregson had taken up the rear. The sniveling nephew stood on a landing at the head of the staircase, shouting and waving a pistol. He fired one shot at me and missed but that was enough for Toby. He sprung at the man and the two of them fell through a large floor-to-ceiling plate glass window into the courtyard two stories below. When we reached them, both of them were dead."

Sherlock Holmes paused and shook his head. "Watson found a large blanket and we wrapped the dog's body in it. We left the culprit's body for Scotland Yard to handle. It seems he had been gambling, lost heavily and set about stealing his aunt's jewelry to pay off his debts.' Gregson gave us one of the police wagons to take Toby home to Pinchin Lane."

"When we reached Mr. Sherman's home, he wiped aside his tears and taking the dog's body carried it to #7 where he laid it in front of Celeste. She sniffed at it, whined and laid down next to it. The puppies scampered around puzzled that their sire was not responding. Later in the morning, Wiggins had performed one of those magic tricks that only he could carry off and gathered all the Irregulars in the small yard behind #7. Each took turns digging the grave for their former comrade. Watson, Mr. Sherman and I joined in.

We gently placed his body in the hole and covered it up. Celeste laid down next to the grave and whimpered. The puppies crawled on top of her. One of the Irregulars had managed to liberate some flowers and laid them on the grave. No one said anything. No eulogies seemed appropriate. We all just looked and finally turned away. When we had completed the burial, I took Mr. Sherman aside and assured him of my continued support for Celeste and the puppies. He started to cry again."

"Celeste died two months later. She was an older dog, probably older than Toby. Sherman, the Irregulars and I buried her next to him. I arranged to have the puppies adopted. A part of my life had come to an end. But now, *(he smiled)* we are back together again, aren't we, old boy?"

The dog barked. Juliet sniffled.

"Oh, as for Mr. Sherman. He died of natural causes. A tough old bird. Now for our test. Watson, let Toby sniff your coat and leave your scarf. Then put the coat on, go downstairs and summon a cab. Ride a mile distant in any direction and dismount. Wait and see if the dog finds you and then both of you come back."

Watson held out the articles of clothing to Toby who sniffed at them, wuffled and wagged his tail. Celeste came over and joined in the sniffing ceremony. Then the doctor patted the dog on the head, donned his coat and said, "Come find me, Toby. You too, Celeste." He left.

The Baroness stared at Holmes. "Could he really find you when he was alive?"

"Oh yes, he located me in a crowded Lambeth park. I was astounded. We'll just have to see if he still has his powers. I wonder about Celeste. She never demonstrated any such skill but she was taken up with the puppies. She could be a tracker, too. Oh, here's Mrs. Hudson!"

A knock on the sitting room door and the landlady appeared. "I just saw Doctor Watson leave, Mr. Holmes. He usually stops in and says goodbye before he goes."

"He'll be back, Mrs. Hudson. He's just taking a short cab ride.'"

She looked puzzled but then noticed the Baroness and Pookie. She did not see Toby or Celeste. "Oh, my goodness, Lady Juliet and Pookie. How lovely to have you back."

"Hello, Martha. I'm not physical any longer or I'd give you a big hug. But it seems you can now see and hear us ghosts. That's wonderful."

Pookie ran toward her and through her. They laughed.

Juliet said, "I heard about my ex-husband, Reginald. Strangled by a fanatic. I lost all affection for him but I certainly didn't want that to happen."

By mutual agreement, Holmes and Mrs. Hudson didn't mention her brief suspicion of the once-corporeal Baroness as Reginald's murderer. Martha was quite ashamed she had mistrusted Juliet. She changed the subject.

"Mr. Holmes, is that dog there your old friend from Lambeth. I've forgotten his name and who is that with him?"

"Yes, Mrs. Hudson. That is Toby, back from the dead and his mate, Celeste. He will be helping us track down a missing person. I'm glad your aversion to dogs has passed on. No pun intended."

"I'm fine with dogs as long as they're ghosts. Pookie and I are great pals, aren't we, dear?"

The Bichon barked.

Holmes laughed. "It's time for our experiment. Toby is going to find Watson. Here, boy, have another sniff of the doctor's scarf. You, too, Celeste. Now, find Watson!"

The two canines sniffed, whined and wagged their tails in agitated fashion, turned and flashed out of the room.

Holmes smiled. "I forgot how rapidly you immortals can move, Baroness. I hope Watson had time to get himself located."

She returned his smile. "We'll see. No, Pookie! You couldn't go with them. You fly better than a bird and fight like a badger but your sense of smell is not your finest trait. Don't you pout at me, miss. We'll just have to wait. Meanwhile, Martha, seen any good plays, lately? That last one was terrible. 'Where's Jane?'

They should have called it 'Who Cares?' It's a shame you can't see any of the Heavenly Theatre Guild's Saintly Spectaculars. Those are wonderful productions. I hesitate to mention that I star in several of them. Now, where are the dogs and the doctor?"

They didn't have to wait long. They interrupted their chat when they heard the tread of Watsons' steps up the staircase and two canine phantoms bounded through the closed door. The Doctor was amazed.

"I rode down Oxford Street and stopped at John Lewis. I was there for only a few minutes when two canine apparitions surrounded me. Toby and Celeste. They found me. Toby hasn't lost any of his skill and Celeste is a hidden wonder. We can certainly use them, Holmes. Baroness, do you have any rewards to give them? They surely deserve it."

Juliet reached into her ghostly reticule, pulled out two large Heavenly Chewies and fed them to the dogs. Pookie looked on crestfallen. "Oh, all right, you pathetic little actress. Here's one for you, too."

The dog was delighted and so was Holmes. The game was apaw.

"Now, where is Mr. Cornhill Jr.? Let's find out."

*****

The Cornhill residence in Mayfair was not quite opulent but well above average in luxury. A three storey, red brick affair surrounded by well-tended gardens and an iron fence that extended around the perimeter spoke of wealth acquired through industry. No nobility or titles here but sufficient money to eschew society and the 'ton.' Not aristocratic, just rich!

The cab with Holmes and Watson turned up to the entrance portico. Flitting along invisibly beside it were Juliet and the three dogs. Invisible, that is, to everyone except the detective and doctor. Watson alit and rang the doorbell and as the butler opened the entryway, the four ghosts floated past him into the foyer. He accepted the two visitor cards and gesturing toward a modest drawing room, said, "Mr. Holmes and Doctor, My name is Matthews. Mrs. Cornhill is in residence and will be with you shortly. She will be joined by her brother-in-law, Mr. John Cornhill. Please be seated. May I offer you tea?"

Holmes, who had little patience for tea-related niceties, thanked him but refused. Watson, as usual had no opportunity to answer. A cup of tea would have gone down favorably. Oh, well!

Juliet and the dogs had settled in by the windows and carefully watched the drawing room door. It opened and a tall, slim, graceful woman in a pea-green dress entered followed by an equally tall gentleman. She had dark hair and brown eyes and a slight similarity to the Baroness. John Cornhill, dressed in a casual tweed suit had grey streaks in his light hair, a small mustache, gold-rimmed spectacles and piercing blue eyes. Neither of them smiled when they greeted the two visitors.

The lady spoke. "Gentlemen, I am Grace Cornhill, Josiah's wife and this is his brother John Cornhill. Thank you for coming and for taking the situation seriously. I must say Scotland Yard has not been particularly helpful. That Inspector Gregson seemed to think my husband has absconded in some sort of dalliance."

Juliet soundlessly choked and Pookie silently growled at the Yard Inspector's name. *"Gregson strikes again. I wonder if Mr. Cornhill is suffering from a case of collateral damage."*

Watson stifled a chuckle.

John Cornhill shook his head. "Jo has been missing for three days now. My father and the company board have been impressed with your reputation and strongly suggested we secure your services. I hope their enthusiasm is not misplaced."

Holmes responded, "At this stage, Mr. Cornhill, I can make no promises but we will exert maximum effort in solving this conundrum."

"Do you believe he is alive? We have had no threats or calls for ransom. Scotland Yard has checked the morgues and major hospitals with no success."

Grace Cornhill bridled. "I refuse to believe he is dead. Perhaps he is wandering about suffering from amnesia. He has never left me and his children like this before."

Holmes asked gently, "Forgive my asking this but I must. Does your husband suffer from any debilitating mental illness? Does he take drugs or heavily imbibe alcohol?"

"Heavens, no!"

John Cornhill intervened. "My brother is remarkably sane and he is as temperate an individual as you will find anywhere. Our father is the soul of disciplined moderation and he has passed that restraint on to his children. No, Mr. Holmes. I'm afraid you will not find him in some opium den or gin joint, at least of his own volition.

"What do you think has happened?"

He paused. "I really don't know. Grace's theory of amnesia is one possibility. I hesitate to speculate on his continued well-being."

Holmes said, "May we see his rooms? I would also like to interview your staff. We plan to look into his offices at Cornhill Enterprises. Are you also employed at the company, Mr. Cornhill?"

"Yes, I'm the Director of Finance."

"Could you arrange for us to interview Josiah Junior's office staff tomorrow morning?"

"Of course. You may wish to speak with my father then. He was eager to meet with you but an important stockholder has taken up his time this afternoon."

"Excellent! You are going to find some of my methods unorthodox. For example, Mrs. Cornhill, may I have a couple of pieces of your husband's clothing that he habitually wears."

"Whatever for?"

"I plan to employ search dogs to look for him. They have a splendid record of uncovering missing individuals."

"Are you serious?"

"You will find, Mrs. Cornhill, that I never jest in pursuit of my commissions. Now, may I see his rooms and meet your staff? Please ask his valet for the appropriate clothing."

During all this, with the exception of Juliet's brief outburst about Inspector Gregson, the celestials and Watson had sat quietly listening to the conversation. It wasn't clear what if anything the dogs were understanding although Pookie seemed to be picking up pieces. She periodically looked at Toby and Celeste, growling meaningfully. The dogs nodded. Watson couldn't believe his eyes or ears. The Baroness kept a knowing smile on her face.

Holmes and Watson rose and Grace Cornhill rang for the butler. "Matthews, please take these gentlemen up to Mr. Josiah's

110

rooms, then call the staff together. Tell Farley that Mr. Holmes wants a sample of the Master's habitual clothing and it has my approval. Mr. Holmes, we will be eagerly awaiting news from you. Please don't disappoint." She tossed her head and strode from the room.

John Cornhill shook their hands and agreed to meet them at ten next morning at Cornhill Enterprises home office. "Thank you gentlemen. No need to tell you. Time is of the essence. I am leaving for the office. If you wish to continue our discussion, I will be at your disposal in the morning."

The Baroness chuckled. *"Why do they all do that? They say, 'There's no need to tell you' Then they tell you anyway. Yes, Mr. Cornhill, we know you want your brother back...or do you?"*

Watson winced and asked telepathically, *"What did you mean by that, Milady?"*

"Oh nothing! Just wondering. Let's go look at rooms. C'mon doggies."

They proceeded up the main staircase to the residence wing with Matthews in the lead. Mr. and Mrs. Cornhill occupied separate but connecting accommodations. She had retired to her rooms. John left for the office. He had his own suite of rooms as did the paterfamilias. Both unoccupied at the moment. Matthews took out a set of keys and unlocked the door to Josiah Jr.'s rooms.

The ghosts floated in. Matthews stood back and gestured for Holmes and Watson to enter. Although a wealthy man, Josiah Jr, did not spend much on personal furnishings or decorations in his apartment. Striped, green wallpaper. A large bed took up the center matched by two armoires, a desk and office chair, a small sofa and a modest bookcase. A connecting door led to Mrs. Cornhill's suite. Locked! Another door led to a bath and WC. Small, inexpensive nature prints on the wall. Several bottles of spirits and a gasogene occupied the top of a sideboard. They opened the armoires whose contents were carefully arranged in precise order.

A knock on the door and a short, well dressed individual entered. Matthews said, "Come in, Farley. Mr. Holmes, Doctor. This is Farley. Mr. Josiah's valet."

"Good morning, gentlemen. How may I be of service?'

"Farley, I would like to have several pieces of Mr. Josiah's habitual outer clothing. They will be returned shortly and intact. Mrs. Cornhill has given her permission."

"A peculiar request, may I say, Mr. Holmes but if Madam has agreed, I'll be happy to comply. Is there anything special you require."

Watson replied. "A scarf or a cravat would do nicely. Something that carries his scent."

"His scent? Forgive me but this sounds like you are planning to use a bloodhound to track the Master."

Holmes looked over at the physically invisible Toby and Celeste. "Not a bloodhound but you are close in your conclusion. We do use dogs."

Both Farley and Matthews simultaneously raised their eyebrows and doubtfully shook their heads. "Of course, sir. Anything that will bring Mr. Josiah back. He is a fine gentleman and is sorely missed by the staff...and of course, his family."

"You were fond of Mr. Cornhill?"

Matthews responded, "We all are. I hope your use of the past tense does not bode ill."

Holmes smiled, "A slip of the tongue. May we have the clothing and then I'd like to meet with you and the rest of the staff. I have some questions about Mr. Cornhill's activities and whereabouts prior to his disappearance. You domestics are probably better able to provide answers than his wife, father or brother. There are children, are there not?"

"Two, a boy and a girl. Both away at school. I'm not sure they know their father is missing."

"Is Mister John married. I saw no sign of a wife or children of his."

"No sir, he is a bachelor. Rather a confirmed one at that. Shall I gather the staff? Besides Farley and myself, there is Mrs. Sunderland, our housekeeper; Gladys, Mrs. Cornhill's maid; Mrs. French, our cook; Sarah and Louise, the upstairs maids; Clive and Charles, our footmen; Jeffers, Mr. Cornhill Senior's valet; Wallace, Mr. John's valet; Gordon, our chauffeur and Williams, the gardener and maintenance man. We supplement the staff whenever the Cornhills socialize. That is not all that frequent. Mr. Cornhill Senior is not fond of parties and such. Mrs. Cornhill conducts afternoon teas when the men are out of the house and she belongs to a Ladies League devoted to London charities."

"Thank you, Matthews. Where shall we meet?"

"The Blue Salon on the ground floor is available. I will summon the staff."

Farley brought out a scarf and two cravats and handed them to Watson. "Mr. Josiah Jr. wears these quite often."

Watson thanked him and surreptitiously passed the articles near the noses of the invisible dogs. Pookie sniffed, too. A bit confusing. They were picking up ambient smells of the members of the household.

Holmes telepathically signaled the baroness. *"Why don't you and the dogs do some investigating. Look for any signs of upset or disruption. Look into the apartments of Mr. John and Mr. Josiah Senior. While you're at it. See what Mrs. Cornhill is up to behind locked doors. We'll be meeting with the staff."*

Juliet shooed the canines out the door and turned toward the other family apartments. Matthews and Farley led Watson and Holmes to the lower floor where the staff was assembling. Matthews took a count and asked, "Where is Gordon?"

One of the maids replied. "Please, Mr. Matthews. Gordon is driving Mr. John down to the Hammersmith buildings."

Holmes clucked his tongue. "That is a shame. He may have been one of the last persons to have seen Mr. Josiah. We'll have to catch up with him when he returns. Can't be helped. Anyway, Ladies and Gentlemen, thank you for interrupting your busy schedules to meet with us. I have just a few questions and we'll let you get back to your assignments. My name is Sherlock Holmes and this gentleman is my associate Doctor John Watson."

One of the footmen, Clive, nudged his counterpart, Charles, and none too softly murmured, "I told you so. Recognized him when he first came in. They're calling in the big guns. They're worried about him being missing."

Holmes, whose hearing is quite acute, looked at the footman and said, "That is correct, Clive is it? Thank you for referring to us as big guns. I prefer to consider ourselves as detectives with long experience. We have been commissioned by the Cornhill family to locate Mr. Josiah Junior who has been gone now for three days. Not a long period of time by itself but we are told it is highly unusual

114

behavior on his part. We are hoping that some of you may be able to shed some light on his disappearance."

More murmuring. Matthews clapped his hands, said nothing but swept his gaze across the group. Silence and then the cook, Mrs. French spoke out. "Mr. Josiah usually stops in the kitchen in the evenin' for a cup of hot cocoa and a few biscuits. Says it helps him sleep. Last time he came by was Monday night. He didn't arrive for breakfast next morning and we haven't seen him since. I hope nothing's happened to the dear man."

The housekeeper, Mrs. Sunderland, said, "I'm sure he's quite all right. This isn't the first time he's gone off for a day or two.

"Mr. Farley, did you help him dress on Tuesday morning?"

"No, sir. He wasn't in his room when I customarily arrived with his morning tea. One of his business suits, shoes, and cane were missing. I assumed he rose early and left without disturbing the house. His coat and hat were gone from the rack at the front door."

"Would he have left without rousing Gordon to drive him to his destination?"

"Mr. Josiah drives his own car, a Wolseley Tonneau. He seldom uses the chauffeured limousine. He leaves it for his father and brother. Mrs. Cornhill uses the estate vehicle when she goes anywhere. Anyway, his auto was gone when I looked for him. You may find it in the company parking garage. Gordon would know."

Matthews turned to the maids. "Sarah and Louise! Have you anything to add?"

They both shook their heads negatively.

"What about you, Jeffers and Wallace. Was Mr. Josiah Junior with his father or brother Monday night?"

Jeffers responded, "As usual, he stopped by to wish his father a good evening. He didn't come into the room. Just stood at the door."

Wallace had nothing to add. The gardener hadn't seen Josiah in days.

"Thank you all. If anything else occurs to you, please let Matthews know and he will contact me immediately." He looked at the butler who nodded agreement. The group disbanded.

Holmes and Watson stood alone in the Blue Salon. "What's our next move, Holmes?"

"I think it's time we paid a visit to Cornhill Enterprises Ltd. But first. let's see what the Baroness and her canine retinue are up to. Let's make sure we are alone. I don't want anyone discovering we have a ghostly cadre assisting us."

Pookie appeared followed by the two trackers. Juliet brought up the rear. *"Well, we discovered precious little in the suites. The upstairs maids had already settled the rooms and the bed linen for the day. Josiah Senior is a most abstemious man. His apartment is more like a monastic cell than a rich man's retreat. John's rooms are more comfortable and well-appointed but we found nothing suspicious. We've all seen Junior's suite."*

"The lady is a different story. Grace Cornhill is quite self-indulgent. In my most flamboyant days, I did not have the vast array of dresses and costumes that she has in three, count them, three large armoires. Her bath chamber is awash (no pun) in toiletries and cosmetics. Keeps her personal maid quite busy. Her husband must be most generous with her. We found her reading a romantic novel. She did not seem overly bothered by Josiah Junior's vanishing. Of course she wasn't aware of us although Pookie was doing her nosiest best to make herself known. She's such an imp."

Holmes smiled. "Matthews just told me that Gordon has returned from taking Mister John to the establishment. He took Josiah Senior there earlier. I want to interview him briefly and then we'll head for the offices. Perhaps, Watson, we can ask him to drive us the eight miles to Hammersmith."

The driver entered the room. "Excuse me, gentlemen. I'm Gordon, the Cornhill's chauffeur. Matthews tells me you wish to speak to me about Mr. Josiah Junior?"

"Yes, Gordon. I'm Sherlock Holmes and this is my associate, Doctor Watson. We have a few questions."

"Blimey, the famous detective and you, Doctor Watson. I've read all your stories. Love them! Are there more coming?"

Watson coughed and looked at Holmes whose opinions of Watson's literary efforts were mixed at best. "I think it's likely, Gordon."

Holmes interrupted. "Is it usual for Mr. Josiah Junior to drive his own car to work?"

"Oh, yes! He loves automobiles. Has his own Wolseley. He leaves me to transport Mr. Josiah Senior and Mr. John in the family limousine. And of course, Mrs. Cornhill in the landau estate car. Mr. John knows how to drive but doesn't like to. Mr. Josiah Senior never learned and doesn't want to. I think he feels it's undignified."

"Did Mr. Josiah Junior leave earlier this morning for the office?"

"I can't rightly say for sure, sir. His car was gone when I came out. I assume he drove to the office."

"Did you see it there when you arrived with Mr. John and Mr. Josiah Senior?"

"No, I didn't. Mr. Josiah Junior keeps it in the company garage and I just left the two gentlemen off at the company entrance and drove back here."

The Baroness exclaimed. *"I think we have to find that car, Holmes. I wonder why he left so early."*

"I agree, Milady. If he went to the office at all."

Watson turned to Gordon and said, "I say, Gordon. I realize you've been out and around all morning. I hope you've had your breakfast?"

"Yes sir. I did. Mrs. French takes good care of us."

"I wonder if we could impose on you to take Mr. Holmes and myself to the Cornhill facilities in Hammersmith?"

"It's no trouble, sir. It's a short ride. Traffic is light at this time. I'll just tell Mr. Matthews. Are you ready to leave now?"

"Yes, I believe we are."

"Won't be a moment." He set out to find the butler.

Juliet and her three ghostly companions sat patiently in the salon. She murmured, *"Call it a woman's intuition but I have suspicions about Mrs. Cornhill. For all the act of dismay she put on for your benefit, she is actually quite blasé about her husband's disappearance. If he's dead, I doubt she actually did him in but I think she knows who did."*

Holmes replied. "Your intuition is often spot on, Baroness. After we're through at Hammersmith, can you flit back here and see what's she's about?'

"The joys of flitting. High speed transportation. Pookie and I will come back. You and our trackers can keep up the search."

Gordon returned. "We'll have to make this quick. Busy day. Mrs. Cornhill wants me to take her out in the estate car a bit later."

Juliet laughed, *"She'll have company."*

*****

Cornhill Enterprises Ltd. consists of several buildings in an industrial park setting surrounded by a tall brick wall and several iron gates. Loud mechanized sounds echoed from a large multi-storey manufacturing facility that dominated the scene. This was offset by a somewhat smaller warehouse and storage area. The entire complex was electrified, powered by a set of petrol-fueled generators. The garage was attached to the warehouse. Several motorized lorries and horse drawn drays were parked around the perimeter. A stable for the wagon horses stood further on. In the middle of the complex sat the glass-enclosed management offices and cafeteria for the workers' daily use. A large black and gold sign sat atop the office building announcing to the world (or at least Hammersmith) that this was the home of the highest quality petrol and steam engine parts and assemblies.

Gordon pulled the Wolseley up to the entrance to the offices, hopped out and opened the doors for Holmes and Watson. The canine cadre and their noble mistress slid off the rear seats and slipped through into a large reception area. A smiling young lady looked at Gordon who introduced the detectives and told her they were there to see Mr. John. She rang a bell and a young page hastened to her desk. "Thank you, Gordon. Oliver, please escort these gentlemen to Mr. John's office."

Gordon turned to Holmes and Watson and said, "Sorry I won't be able to pick you back up, gentlemen. As I told you, I must take Mrs. Cornhill out to her club meeting and bring her back."

Juliet snorted. *"Aha. A club meeting. I wonder who will be there?"*

Watson laughed telepathically. *"Don't let your misgivings run away with you, Milady."*

She retorted. *"Just you wait, Doctor. My intuition never fails. Meanwhile, we need to turn these dogs loose. Do you still have the scarf and cravats?"*

"Yes, but I can't show them right now without raising suspicions. This page boy will wonder what I'm doing waving articles of clothing around in midair."

Oliver was a talkative but well-spoken sort. He ran a monologue as he guided them up a flight of stairs. "Welcome to Cornhill Enterprises Ltd. The automotive future is here behind these walls. Do you gentlemen drive? No? It's still a bit difficult with all the ridiculous laws in place. Not too long ago, you needed a team of men carrying flags to warn the public of a self-propelled vehicle. There's a new Motor Car Act proposed in Parliament. It will replace the Locomotives on Highways Act of 1896 which had increased the speed limit for motorcars to 14 mph from the previous 4 mph in rural areas and 2 mph in towns. Hopefully, they'll remove the limit altogether. If you're going to drive, you'll have to get a license. No test! Anyone with five shillings can get one. I guess it would help if you knew what you were doing. And oh yes! Your car has to have a unique identifying number on display. I hope you learn to drive and get an auto. We could use the business." He laughed. "Here we are, gentlemen. This is Paula. She's Mr. John's secretary."

The executive area was laid out in marble and mahogany. Behind a substantial desk sat another attractive young lady. In hiring assistants, someone had an eye for feminine good looks. Two trays and a typewriter occupied her desktop. A Bell telephone sat atop a separate table next to her chair.

"Thank you Oliver. You must be Mr. Holmes and Doctor Watson. Mr. John told me to expect you. He's just finishing up a meeting. Won't you step into the anteroom? Shall I order up some tea?"

Before Holmes could refuse, Watson thanked her and accepted. Juliet laughed. She reached into her ethereal reticule and fed three Heavenly Chewies to the dogs. Pookie finished hers, slipped down, put her invisible paws on the young lady's knees and stared into her face. When there was no response, she padded back to Juliet, flopped down and pouted. The Baroness ruffled her fur. *"She can't see, hear or smell you, Pookie. I keep telling you. You're a ghost as are Toby and Celeste. That's a big advantage when you're in the sleuthing business. You can go anywhere and watch anyone without them knowing. We're going to go look for Mr. Josiah's car in a little while and nobody will notice us. Maybe we'll find Mr. Josiah. I hope he's still alive."*

The door to the inner office opened and two men in shirtsleeves exited carrying large binders and brief cases. John Cornhill stepped out behind them and nodded at Holmes and Watson. "Gentlemen, good morning. Just reviewing the finances of a new acquisition. Do you have any news for me?"

Holmes shook his head in the negative.

"Paula, call over to Father's office and see if he's available. He's eager to meet you. This new merger is occupying most of our time. My brother is Director of Production and was deeply into the mechanics of bringing several manufacturing processes together when he disappeared. We've had to temporize with the management of our tentative partner. It's essential that he be found swiftly and brought back. The business depends on it."

The secretary hung up her telephone apparatus and said, "Your Father is busy but will be available shortly. She smiled at Watson. I'll have the tea sent to his office."

John walked out of the anteroom, turned and said, "In the meantime, I'll fetch Jo's chief engineer and his technical manager. I don't know whether they can shed any light on the situation. Paula, will you call Hopkins and Somerfield."

She reached for her telephone again, had a short conversation and said, "They're coming."

Hopkins, the chief engineer, was a short, rotund individual with a flushed complexion. A knot of dark brown hair tumbled over his forehead. He wore gold-rimmed spectacles. He was in his shirtsleeves and looked as if he had slept in his clothes. In fact, he had. They were working all hours to initiate the transitions to the new processes brought about by the upcoming merger. He looked exhausted. Somerfield, the technical manager, was clad in a grease stained coverall. He was tall, lanky and bald. Both were clean shaven or would be if it were not for incipient stubble on their jaws.

John introduced the detective and the doctor. Celeste sniffed at them and was put off by Somerfield's body odor. As was Juliet. Hopkins stifled a yawn and said, "Excuse us, gentlemen. We've been tied up testing a new milling machine. It's been giving us fits but it will be a key component in our new production line. We don't always look and smell this scruffy. What can we do for you?"

Holmes smiled and said, "Machines have minds of their own, don't they? We are looking into the disappearance of Mr. Josiah Junior. Can you shed any light on the subject."

Smithfield scratched his head. "Wish we could. We need him to make some important decisions. Last time I saw him, it was Monday evening. He was going home in his car but said he'd be back later in the night. He had some business back at his house he had to attend to. Last we saw of him. Funny thing, though. His car is back in the warehouse garage. Don't know how long it's been there."

Hopkins frowned. "I hope he's all right. We certainly could use him right now."

Paula interrupted. "Mr. John, your Father is available now.

"Follow me. His office is on the top floor. Actually, it is the top floor. A penthouse. Father is a rather solemn, no-nonsense gentleman but an excellent businessman. Cornhill Enterprises owes its growth and stature to his splendid initiatives and management guidance. He is a forward looking entrepreneur but a social traditionalist and political conservative. Might I suggest that you do not mention your intention to use search dogs to seek out Jo. Where are they, by the way?"

"They are with their trainer. We will be calling on them a bit later."

Juliet winced to herself, *"Lady Juliet Armstrong, former Baroness Crestwell – ghostly dog trainer! Mr. Sherman would love that. So would Raymond. Actually, these dogs don't need training. They're wonders."*

They reached the penthouse floor. Floor to ceiling windows. Like the rest of the building, electric lights added to the illumination. A slightly larger administrative desk manned (womaned?) by a somewhat prettier secretary. Somewhat more radiant smile. More expensive typewriter. Three Bell telephones on a fancier table. The pecking order was clear.

123

"Good morning, Mr. John, Mr. Holmes and Doctor Watson. A pleasure to meet you. Mr. Josiah Senior is in his office. Please go in."

She rose and opened the door to a sparsely furnished, dimly lit management office. A large, uncluttered desk with an equally large executive chair, faced by three plain but comfortable smaller seats, a sofa, two sideboards on which rested two stock tickers. Farther on, a conference table with more chairs. Photographs of the company's products and production machinery filled two walls. No trophies, awards or other symbols.

The great man was seated at his desk reading a document. He did not rise or acknowledge anyone for what seemed like an eternity. He waved his hand in their general direction, an obvious signal to be seated. Finally, he looked up, first at John and then at Holmes and Watson. He frowned and said one word, "Well?"

John spoke, "Father, this is Mr. Sherlock Holmes and Doctor Watson."

"I assumed as much. Your fame precedes you, gentlemen and our board recommends you but I am more interested in what you are going to do today to restore my son to his position in this business. This is a critical moment for Cornhill Enterprises and his absence is ill-timed. Extremely ill-timed! You have your commission. Find him!"

Juliet winced. *"So much for paternal concern and affection."* She was sitting on one of the sideboards sharing space with a clattering stock ticker.

Holmes looked at the patriarch and asked. 'Do you have any suggestions as to his whereabouts?"

"No!"

"Then we will initiate our search."

"I should hope so. Keep John informed. John, where are we on the merger transfer costs?"

*****

Holmes, Watson and the invisibles found themselves back down in the reception area once again in the care of the loquacious Oliver. "How can I assist you, gentlemen?"

"A tour of the facilities would be most welcome, Oliver."

"Nothing easier. I'll get Ellen. She conducts our guided tours. Please wait here."

When they stood alone, Watson took the opportunity to once more pass the scarf and cravats in front of the dogs' ghostly noses and said "Good boy, Toby. Good girl, Celeste. Go find Mr. Josiah."

The canines whuffed, wagged their otherworldly tails and bounded out of the lobby heading for the plant and warehouse.

Juliet patted Pookie and said, *"You and I are going for a flit, my girl. I want to see what Grace Cornhill is up to. Let's see if I can remember how to get back to Mayfair."*

Pookie barked, back flipped and headed off out the door.

"Ah, so you recall. Clever doggie. You're just as smart as those two trackers."

Oliver returned with yet another blonde beauty this time in a black and gold uniform topped by a jaunty cap. "Mr. Holmes, Doctor Watson, this is Ellen. She is the Cornhill Tour Guide. She'll be happy to take you wherever you wish to go."

The young lady smiled. "Good morning. I understand you are searching for Mr. Josiah Junior. I don't believe he is here on the

125

site but let us make the rounds just to be sure. He may be in the plant or in the design center with the engineers. He often comes in very early before reception opens. Of course, he has his own keys to the entire facility. Let's go to the plant first. Please stay with me. Some of the areas are dangerous with sheet metal presses, coating vats, milling machines and the like. Walkways are carefully marked. We haven't lost a visitor yet. I certainly wouldn't want to suffer the loss of two famous people like you. She laughed."

"As you know, Cornhill Enterprises manufactures parts and entire assemblies for petrol and steam powered vehicles. As I understand it, we will shortly be merging with an as yet secret company to produce entire automobiles and lorries. Part of that work will be done here and part at our partner's location. I believe Mr. Josiah Junior is in charge of planning that arrangement."

"I'm sorry but we're about to go through an area of very loud noises. There are signs posted identifying the different processes. I'll be happy to answer your questions when we can once more hear ourselves think and talk. Most of the workers wear earplugs. I have some if you wish them." She held out a small bag.

Watson took a set but Holmes as usual, forbore.

They entered a large industrial door to the sounds of heavy stamping machinery, rolling conveyors, roaring furnaces and finished metallic pieces clattering and falling into bins. Watson nudged Holmes. Sniffing around the work stations were the two members of the heavenly canine cadre. Neither seemed excited. Of course, Ellen couldn't see them.

The dogs padded down the walkway, stopping periodically to sniff at a machine or a worker. Suddenly they both paused in front of a stamping press. Something was attracting their attention. Being bodiless, they climbed over the moving device and sniffed at a bin. They turned to Holmes and barked.

Holmes grabbed Ellen's arm and shouted, "Stop this machine – NOW!"

He reached over to the worker standing next to the press and repeated his cry. The man looked dubious but when Ellen frantically waved her arms, he reached over and pulled a switch. The noise of the stamper ceased but was immediately replaced by the sound of Ellen's scream. Peeking out from the pile of unfinished piston rings in the deep bin was the sleeve of a tweed jacket. They had found Josiah Junior.

*****

Two hours later, Inspector Gregson, Holmes, Watson, John Cornhill, two members of the Cornhill security staff and several constables watched as the medical examiner did his preliminary review. The factory floor manager and foreman were standing by. Production had ground to a halt. Ellen had been sent to the company's medical facility. She had fainted at the discovery of the body.

John Cornhill identified his brother. The doctor (somewhat obviously) proclaimed the victim to be dead - probably for several days. It looked like strangulation. There were post mortem bruises on the body from being dumped in the bin and having piston rings dropped on it but no wounds other than a neck fracture. A murder! Thankfully, it had not been subjected to the stamping process. The inspector agreed with Holmes that the killer had taken the inert body and dumped it in one of the many empty wheeled bins stored in the warehouse garage. Eventually, the bins were towed out to the factory floor and the production stations.

Gregson questioned the foreman. The parts bins were brought in and filled with finished product several times a day. They were then taken to the next station where the rings were removed and attached to the pistons and then on to larger assemblies. Once a bin was emptied it was returned to the warehouse garage to await another round. It usually sat for a few days. Josiah's Wolseley was parked in the garage near an array of empty bins. No one saw the body deep in the container when it was set up at the piston ring station.

The Yard detective looked at Holmes quizzically. "How did you know the body was in the bin?"

"Judgement mixed with intuition, Inspector. Over time, one develops a sixth sense about such things." Gregson was dubious but as usual, lacked any sharp rejoinder. Holmes was hardly going to mention that Toby and Celeste were still on the job in spite of passing on to the hereafter. He and Watson silently praised the dogs and promised them a large ration of Heavenly Chewies when Lady Juliet returned to the Meadows. Part one of the mission accomplished! Josiah was found. Part two was yet to come. Who killed him?

Cornhill Senior was informed by John of the unfortunate discovery. His reactions were typical of the man. Brief shock, followed by concern for the merger and irritation that the police had shut down the production process for the day. He told the factory manager to have the staff work an extra shift to make up for the lost time. He summoned Holmes and Watson to his penthouse office.

"I suppose you consider your commission is satisfied with the discovery of my son's body. No such thing. I want you to find the culprit or culprits responsible for this and prevent any further damage. Whoever they are, they've come close to scuttling our new business venture. I can only hope Josiah's assistants are capable of carrying out the transition."

Watson was dismayed at the old man's single-minded absorption with business and apparently uncaring attitude toward the loss of a son. "I've seen this type before, Holmes but I can never get over the cold-blooded nature of these tycoons. Unforgiveable. Are you going to pursue this or leave it to Scotland Yard?"

"I share your distaste, Watson, but I think we have some obligation to see this thing to its end. So, yes, I plan to stay with it. The Baroness, you, me, and the dogs. I suppose by now, Josiah's wife has been informed. I wonder how she is taking it."

Unaware of the grisly discovery at the plant, the Baroness and Pookie had flitted back to the Cornhill manse in Mayfair. She heard the news when she arrived in Grace Cornhill's suite.

"Gladys, Mr. John just called. Mr. Josiah is dead. I shall have to take on the role of grieving widow. I suppose I shall have to go into mourning. Briefly! I'm certainly not going to do it for two years. Such a bother. Black is definitely not my color. Call Mrs. Sunderland and Matthews. We must prepare the house. The old man will no doubt demand it although he cares not a whit for either of his sons or me either for that matter. He mourns when the value of Cornhill shares drops."

Mrs. Sunderland entered the room. "My deepest condolences, Mrs. Cornhill. I was quite fond of Mr. Josiah Junior."

"Yes, yes, Thank you Mrs. Sunderland. You and Matthews must get the house in order. Contact the undertaker and make arrangements for getting the police to release the body and transfer it here and prepare for a viewing. No doubt, we will be inundated with hypocrites coming to sympathize with the old man. As if he cares. This will put paid to his merger plans at least for a while. John can work with the undertaker and vicar to organize the funeral. We will have to inform the press."

Matthews arrived. The housekeeper listed off the initial steps to be taken in the home:

Draw the curtains and stop the clocks at the time of his death. We don't know exactly when he died. We'll have to estimate.

Cover the mirrors throughout the house and turn family photos and portraits face down.

All the servants must wear a black ribbon.

Procure a wreath of laurel and yew or boxwood, tied with black crepe or ribbons, and hang it on the front door. The undertaker will know how and where.

The bell knob or door handle must also be draped with black crepe and tied with a ribbon.

Mr. John will no doubt have the plant site and offices suitably draped and the employees called upon to demonstrate their regrets.

Grace shook her head impatiently. "Fine, fine! Well, get to it. I guess I won't be able to go to my club today. Nothing for it, I suppose. Drat! John should be on his way home by now."

Juliet listened to this, fascinated. She wondered whether her husband Reginald went to all this trouble when she was killed. She was also dismayed at the wife's attitude. Clearly, this was not a happy home. Or was it more than that? Was it a perilous home? Her suspicions were aroused. She looked at the dog.

The Bichon cocked her head and stared at the Baroness. A Heavenly Chewy would go down well right about now.

"Pookie, we need to get back to Mr. Holmes. I wonder how he is progressing. There is more here than meets the eye. But let's wait a bit and see what happens next."

*****

Holmes, Watson, Gregson and the two ethereal dogs had taken over a conference room in the executive offices. John Cornhill had excused himself but not before both Toby and Celeste had thoroughly sniffed him. He was wearing a cologne that caused the dogs to sneeze.

The medical examiner had departed with the body to conduct a post mortem and Gregson had stationed constables around the factory floor and the warehouse. The stamping machine and the bin in which the victim was found was impounded and that part of the plant blocked off. The police gave no indication as to when the ban would be lifted. The factory manager, foreman and ultimately Cornhill Senior were not at all pleased.

Holmes looked at Watson and Gregson. "Let us go to the warehouse garage. I want to examine Josiah's auto and the surrounding bins." He beckoned the two dogs who bounded out in front. Somehow they knew where the detective was heading.

The warehouse was typical of its kind. Well lit. On one side were stacks of finished goods packaged for transportation and delivery. Raw materials – sheet steel, wire, assortments of nuts, bolts, screws and other fasteners took up the center. Bins of coal and coke for the furnaces stood ready to be wheeled onto the factory floor through a set of passageways. Several vehicles were parked somewhat randomly in the open interior. One of those was Josiah Cornhill's Wolseley Tonneau.

Unbeknownst to Gregson, the dogs climbed over the upholstered seats front and rear. They sniffed at the driver's position, steering wheel, pedals and levers and the storage baskets, even the engine under the bonnet. Something was disturbing them. The Inspector looked at Holmes and Watson. "A very nice auto but I don't see anything remarkable, do you?"

Holmes murmured under his breath. "You see but you do not observe." Aloud he said. "I'll want to study it further before I say anything definitive. (Translation: The dogs are on to something.)"

Suddenly Celeste had a fit of sneezing. Holmes led her back to the factory floor where the bin that had contained the body still stood. He guided each of the canines over to the bin and watched. Celeste and Toby both sneezed again, this time repeatedly. He telepathically announced. *"Watson, I think we have it."*

*****

Grace Cornhill paced back and forth in her boudoir. She sent Gladys off to assist Matthews and Mrs. Sunderland in organizing the staff and preparing the house for mourning. She pouted. "Where was John? He should be here by now." She had sent Gordon to pick him up.

She heard the car approach the front door and stood waiting for his arrival. He strode in, climbed the stairs two at a time, entered the room and closed the door behind him. He walked over and embraced her, kissing her passionately. Juliet was thunderstruck. (but not shocked, she was shocking but never shocked!) *"Ooh Pookie, What have we here?"*

Grace squirmed out of his grip. "Not now! We have to be careful. Is everything all right?"

"I'm not sure. That damn detective and his medical colleague are making me nervous. That idea of yours to involve them and put the police off the scent may not have been as clever as we thought."

"Don't tell me you're losing your nerve. What made you use wires from the car? Why ever did you dump his body in a parts bin of all places?"

"First things I could find. I used the bin because someone was moving around in the warehouse. They might have seen me."

"At two in the morning?"

"We're all working odd hours getting ready for the merger. I expected to retrieve the body and dump it in the Thames later but they moved the bin and just today sent it on to the stamping machine. I couldn't find it. That fool Holmes discovered it but there's no way he can tie it back to me."

The Baroness scowled, *"Don't be too sure of that, my lad!"*

Mrs. Cornhill frowned, "Holmes is a lot of things but he's not a fool. That Scotland Yard inspector doesn't seem too bright. Let's hope he takes over the investigation."

"I'll see to that. I'll go to the office and get Father to terminate Holmes' commission. He hates to waste money."

"Do it now! Well, Junior is out of the way. Senior is next. Then we'll sell the business to our prospective partners and live a life of leisure on the Riviera. How do we get rid of the old man?"

"Slow poison. Wasting away at the death of his older son. Overcome with sorrow."

"Are you serious? He doesn't have a sentimental bone in his body."

"Leave it to me. I know his weak spots. We'll have to wait a bit. It will look suspicious if he dies too soon after his son's passing."

"Not too long! I can't stand him or this place. I'll have to tell the brats in school their father is dead. I'm not sure they'll care very much. They seldom saw him. Now get out of here. Go see your father and be careful. The servants are a nosey lot."

Juliet grinned, *"They're not the only ones, Grace. Let's go, Pookie. Holmes needs to know."*

*****

Back at the Cornhill Enterprises conference room, Sherlock Holmes and Watson sat alone. Holmes was in a quandary. How was he going to confront John Cornhill based on sneezing ethereal dogs. His cologne was the key. He was guilty. Of that Holmes was certain but he had to convince Gregson and obtain incontrovertible proof. He, Watson and the Baroness would have to contrive a trap but how. There were no apparent witnesses. From what the medical examiner said the strangulation was done with a rope or wire.. The marks on his neck confirmed that. But where was the garrote? They had searched the bin. Nothing. The car was clean but probably could stand another search. It's still impounded along with the bin.

As they were about to return to the warehouse garage, the Baroness and Pookie flitted in. *"I have news, Holmes. Pookie and I witnessed a tryst between Grace and John. The grieving widow is a femme fatale. She and her brother-in-law contrived between the two of them to kill Josiah Junior and they plan to do in the patriarch, inherit the spoils and then sell off their ownership in the company. They'll then do a bunk to the Riviera."*

The detective smiled. "That confirms it. Our wonder dogs identified John as the killer from the cologne he wears. But I need tangible evidence to prove his guilt and her complicity. Watson and I are going back to the scene of the crime and scouring once again for evidence. Gregson has left and he has released most of the constables. He's at the morgue with the medical examiner. I doubt if he'll find anything but we'll see. He'll be back in about an hour. They've started up the production line again. Watson, see if you can get a hold of Messrs. Hopkins or Somerfield. We need someone who is expert on the innards of a Wolseley Tonneau. It's a shame Gordon is not here."

Juliet spoke up. *"He could be. Due to the death, Grace Cornhill had to cancel her club meeting, if that's where she was going. Gordon may be available. Ask Paula to call the house and see if he can come back here. The poor man must feel like a jumping jack shuttling back and forth."*

Watson went off and returned shortly. Neither Hopkins nor Somerfield were familiar with the car, though they certainly wished they could be. Gordon was indeed engaged but would be on hand shortly. He had just dropped Matthews off at the undertakers and was on his way out to the Hammersmith site with Mr. John. He knew all there was to know about the Wolseley Rear Entry Tonneau.

Holmes turned to the Glamorous Ghost. "When you and the dogs get back to the Meadows make sure Mr. Sherman has a wonderful treat in store for them. They've done a marvelous job. Toby seems to have slipped back into the tracking process as if he never left it. I'm especially impressed with Celeste. She is a major surprise. I don't suppose you could talk Raymond into letting them cross the Rainbow Bridge and slip into Heaven. They could stay with you."

Juliet laughed, *"First, I'd have to fight off Mr. Sherman and his staff and second, I doubt if the dogs would want to leave the*

Meadows. They have all of their canine friends there. Pookie sneaks out to join them every chance she gets. No, Holmes. They're happier where they are. They're the Canine Cadre. I plan to visit the Meadows on a regular basis. I can see becoming good friends with Mr. Sherman and his aides. It's a fun place. Oh, here's Gordon."

"Hello, Mr. Holmes. I'm back again. What can I do for you and the Doctor? I just left Mr. John off. He's going to see Mr. Josiah Senior. Poor man! Lost his older son."

The Baroness laughed sardonically, *"As if he cares!"*

Holmes said, "Gordon, I need your expertise. I have reason to believe Mr. Josiah's Wolseley Tonneau was involved in his death. I need someone, you, to examine the car and tell me if you see anything unusual or out of the ordinary."

"Sure, I'd be happy to. Let's take a look. I doubt if we'll find anything. Mr. Josiah Junior treated that automobile like it was a treasure. Always fussing over it."

They walked out to the warehouse garage. Unseen, the dogs and Juliet accompanied them. Pookie jumped into the driver's seat and Toby and Celeste once again nosed at the storage baskets. Celeste had another fit of sneezing.

Gordon sat down on top of the Bichon. She climbed up invisibly onto his lap. "Mr. Holmes, let's start her up. I'll turn on the spark and the fuel. Would you give the crank a few turns, please."

Holmes spun the crank. Nothing happened. Watson examined the fuel tank. Almost full. They tried again. Gordon gave it one more try and then broke out laughing. "This little beauty isn't going anywhere. Two of the ignition cables are gone."

"Gone?"

"Gone and one is in backwards. I don't understand it. He couldn't have driven the car without them. Someone has been playing fast and loose. I can't imagine it was Mr. Josiah."

"Neither can I, Gordon. Neither can I. Watson, let's see if Gregson is back yet."

Toby barked. He was sniffing at a rattan storage case hung on the right side of the rear seat. A similar but smaller bag was attached to the left and Celeste was nosing at it. Watson said, "We looked in there before. Some spare parts and cables. Oh…cables!"

Holmes opened the bags. Spark plugs, a large oil can and two cables that matched the ignition wires that were still installed. The other contained a picnic basket, table cloths, napkins and dishes. Celeste tried to bite a napkin.

Gordon looked at the parts bag and said. "Well, these cables are useless. You can see the connectors are split and broken off."

Inspector Gregson strolled into the garage with his Sergeant. "Is this a meeting of the Royal Auto Club or have you found something?"

Watson chuckled, "Would you believe the murder weapon or weapons."

"What?"

Holmes pointed to the cables. "Behold, Inspector. I think if you take these cables and place them against the marks on Josiah's neck and throat, you'll find a match. If you also check the skin on Mr. John Cornhill's hands, you will find abrasions caused by the rough outer surface of these wires. He is your murderer. He is with his Father right now, probably trying to get me relieved of my commission. If you hurry, you can also catch his partner in crime. Mrs. Cornhill."

"Josiah's wife? Blimey! And you know all this, how?"

"All will be revealed, Gregson but I think you'll want to apprehend your culprits first."

"Right, Sergeant. Get whatever constables we have left and come with me up to the executive penthouse. You too, Holmes and Watson."

The Baroness and dogs needed no invitation. Gordon tagged along.

*****

Josiah Senior was livid. "Are you out of your mind, Gregson. Arresting my son for murdering his brother. Ridiculous! And you, too, Holmes. John is right. I never should have hired you."

"Mr. Cornhill, I believe we have sufficient evidence to hold your son and daughter-in-law for questioning and I am going to take them into custody. (He hoped he was correct.)

"Nonsense. I'll see you're charged with false arrest. Do you realize how you're disrupting our merger activities? Holmes, you'll pay for this."

Gordon interrupted. "Excuse me, Sir, but I thought you should know. Matthews ordered me to return to the house immediately. Mrs. Cornhill is leaving unexpectedly. She wants to go to the train station and journey to Liverpool. She is booked on the White Star Celtic that is leaving tomorrow for New York. I'm to go to the house right away."

Gregson said, "You will not be alone. I'll be with you. Sergeant, detain Mr. John Cornhill."

John shook his head. "She's betraying me. The witch! I loved her."

Holmes looked at the patriarch and said, "I think you may wish to retract your threats, sir."

The old man blustered and then seemed to collapse in on himself.

*****

The next day they gathered together once again.

Gregson shook his head. "She's setting up John Cornhill to hang. She said he seduced her and forced her to condone the killing of her husband, Josiah Junior. I'm not sure what will become of her. She's certainly an accessory. The woman is like the spider – a Black Widow."

"What about the children?"

"There's an aunt. Josiah Senior has agreed to support them. He's going ahead with the merger without his two sons. He's a single minded profit driven autocrat."

The Inspector took up his hat and coat and left.

Holmes turned to the Baroness. "Once again your intuition was spot on. I congratulate you."

"Don't congratulate me. It's the dogs you should be praising. The Canine Cadre. They're back with Mr. Sherman and a big doggie celebration is planned. Pookie is included. I'm going to spend some time with Martha and then go back to my celestial villa. I think I'll put the Meadows on my frequent visit agenda. Good bye, Doctor Watson. This may be the last time we get together, Holmes."

"Oh, I doubt that, Milady."

She giggled, "So do I."

The Clamorous Ghosts

Lady Juliet Armstrong, former Baroness Crestwell, now deceased, took a sip from her cup of Ambrosia as she sat in a bower in the Meadows with Mr. Sherman and his caretaker team. They were the group charged with managing the vast expanses where departed animals relaxed and gamboled, some preparing to cross the Rainbow Bridge to Paradise – some not, but all enjoying their comfortable stay.   She and Pookie had made another of what was now becoming routine excursions to the Meadows. She enjoyed the visits no end ever since she was first introduced to the giant park by Mr. Raymond.

Pookie had run off and joined her canine colleagues in a complex game of multidimensional fetch. Juliet didn't understand the rules but clearly the animals did. Once again, Toby and Celeste, the tracking wonder dogs were acting as referees and once again Marshall was standing on the sidelines barking protests at the calls. Situation normal.

The current assistants at the Meadows were Charles, Lucia, Astrophel and Daria. Charles and Lucia were deceased volunteers on rotating duty. Astrophel and Daria were angels. They had just finished discussing how many of the war horses killed in the Second Boer War were being reunited with their riders and brought across the Rainbow Bridge.

"Wars are terrible " said Lucia. "I've often wondered why the Almighty allows them to happen."

Astrophel replied. "Mankind has free will. They can do awful things with it. I remember the American Civil War. We were flooded with victims - men, women, children, horses and other animals. Many of the horses are still here. I hope we never have to live with that again."

Juliet agreed, sighed, finished her Ambrosia and said, "I must return to Paradise. The Heavenly Theatre Guild is rehearsing another Saintly Spectacular. It's called 'Heaven's Above' (not a very original title) and I have a lead. So does Pookie. We will visit again shortly. I really appreciate our time together."

Mr. Sherman laughed, "So do we, Baroness. So do we. Come back soon. We're expanding the equine field to accommodate all the newly arrived horses. I know you love the ponies."

Juliet called over to Pookie who had just scored some kind of complex goal. Marshall as usual was protesting. "Come on, girl. We have to flit over the Bridge. The theatre calls."

The Bichon was unhappy at having to leave while her team was ahead but executed a parting backflip and joined the Baroness. Juliet laughed. "You're such a showoff, Pookie. I hope you've learned your part in the show."

The dog dropped in mid-flit and took up the pace walking on her hind legs, spinning and waving her paws.

"Fine, now all I have to do is remember my lines and sing my two songs."

They reached the baronial mansion and entered.

They floated into the rooms of her ethereal chateau. Elegantly decorated in muted colors but dominated by her signature scarlet, the celestial villa reflected her personality. Beautiful flowers bloomed eternally throughout the house, filling it with riotous color and otherworldly fragrances.

Heavenly Real Estate had done a marvelous job of designing and 'constructing' her perpetual home. With a flick of her evanescent fingers, she could change the colors, shapes, furnishings and dimensions of her property from small and cozy to boundless – as the mood suited her. Each estate in Heaven took up no space at all but simultaneously stretched into infinity.

Equally, the dog could summon snug dens, grassy dells or sprawling expanses lined with restful cushions. Doggie toys and snacks were in abundance. Ghostly sheep, squirrels and cats appeared on command, ready to be chased. And then, there was always the Meadows.

As she and Pookie passed through the doorway, Juliet became aware that they had company coming. Four women were advancing on the portal with determined steps. "Who was this?" She was about to find out.

The four wraiths were clothed in white robes decorated with violet and green rosettes. The obvious leader was clearly a dowager of a certain age. She was accompanied by three younger but mature women. The dowager spoke.

"I am addressing the former Baroness Crestwell, am I not."

"You are indeed, madam. May I ask who you are?"

"I am Letitia Forsythe, former Duchess of Ailesworth. These gentlewomen are respectively, Lady Agnes Faulkner, former Countess of Durham; Viscountess Sarah Wellington and Miss Penelope Swift. As you have probably observed from our dress, we are emeritus members of the Women's Social and Political Union (WSPU) dedicated to advancing women's suffrage. Our colors, green, white and violet stand for '**G**ive **W**omen the **V**ote."

Penelope interrupted. "But more importantly at this moment, we constitute the Committee for the Release of Lady Dorothy Fletcher (the CRLDF). She is currently being held by the

Police in London on suspicion of terrorism. It is a complete fabrication based on prejudice and bias against women. Lady Dorothy has done nothing wrong."

The Countess and Viscountess vociferously and loudly agreed. "She must be released and her good name restored. We demand justice."

The Duchess frowned. "Thank you, Penelope. Thank you ladies." She turned to Juliet and said "That is why we are here. We require your assistance."

The Baroness gulped. Pookie was observing all of this with her head cocked to one side, puzzled.

"Ladies, I strongly support the Suffragist movement although I must say, I have some doubts about the Pankhursts and their campaigns.'

The Countess intervened. "Emmeline Pankhurst and her daughters Christabel and Sylvia are troublemakers with their aggressive tactics and hunger strikes. They can get themselves into difficulties without even trying. Lady Dorothy Fletcher is a peaceable soul who wouldn't harm a flea and yet they're blaming her for plotting to bomb Parliament. Sheer nonsense."

"I was about to say that while I fully sympathize, I don't see what I can do to help."

The Viscountess blurted, "Not you! Sherlock Holmes!"

The Duchess took back command. "We were present at the recent Garden Party arranged by the UK branch of the Celestial Sisterhood when you told of the attempt at bombing the Queen at Windsor Castle. You spoke of Mr. Holmes' role in bringing the culprit to book. The villain shot himself, didn't he? We want you to get Mr. Holmes to take Lady Dorothy's case and get her exonerated."

Juliet blanched. "I think I warned all of you that story was confidential and not to be repeated. I regret having mentioned it. Me and my big mouth!"

"We're not interested in talking about Her Majesty's near miss. We want Mr. Holmes to clear Lady Dorothy."

She thought she had an out. "I'll need Mr. Raymond's permission to get in touch with Sherlock Holmes again. He is reluctant to have me spending all my time back in London and beyond."

The Countess replied, "We know. We've already spoken to Raymond. In fact he's coming now."

She looked out and saw a figure she recognized all too well, approaching. A middle-aged male, tall, dressed in morning *(mourning?)* clothes, clean shaven, not a hair out of place, dark eyes, color undetermined. He seemed to be floating inches above the ground. Mr. Raymond, a Senior Celestial Director, charged with keeping Paradise in heavenly shape and keeping the Baroness and Pookie in tow.

"Good afternoon, ladies," he intoned. "Another heavenly day but then they all are."

"Enough small talk, Raymond." The Duchess bellowed. "Are you or aren't you going to allow Baroness Crestwell to convince Sherlock Holmes to free Lady Dorothy Fletcher from her vile imprisonment?"

Her three companions joined in loudly urging him, completely ignoring whether Juliet wanted to comply. She looked at Pookie and shrugged.

"Ladies, it is not Heaven's policy to interfere with the workings of the worldly authorities."

"Oh, balderdash, Raymond. We know otherwise."

Juliet agreed with the old lady. She had interfered more times than she could remember. Actually, she wouldn't at all mind getting back with Holmes, Watson and Mrs. Hudson.

He hemmed and hawed. "I suppose, in the interest of justice we could suspend the rules, once again."

That sealed it.

The Baroness looked at the Clamorous Ghosts. "Why don't you describe the situation to me. You know, I can't guarantee Holmes will take the case."

Penelope let up a cheer. "Oh. he will. I just know he will. Tell her, Your Grace."

The Duchess cleared her throat. "Lady Fletcher is a Marchioness. She initially was a member of the National Union of Women's Suffrage Societies (NUWSS) and later joined Emmeline Pankhurst's Women's Social and Political Union (WSPU). She marched, helped prepare materials and otherwise was a good soldier but hardly a firebrand."

"Unfortunately, she was married to an Irishman who at one time had been a captain in the Fenians. He was killed in 1898 in an unsuccessful attempt to repeat the infamous 1867 bombing of Clerkenwell Prison that killed 12 people and injured 120. The Home Office and Scotland Yard uncovered yet another bombing plan this past year. This time the target was Parliament. An anonymous informer accused several men and one woman, Lady Dorothy, now remarried to a Marquess."

"She was charged with abetting the planned attack in order to advance not the Irish cause but the goals of the Suffragist movement. Sheer nonsense! The only evidence against her was the informant's accusation. But it was enough for the muddle headed police. We need the talents of Sherlock Holmes to put paid to the accusation. The Marchioness is currently in Holloway Prison."

Juliet looked at Raymond who shrugged and stared sheepishly off in space. "I suppose Pookie and I could make another trip to London but only after we have made arrangements with The Heavenly Theatre Guild. They are not going to be happy to use our understudies.

Raymond smiled. "Pookie has an understudy?"

"Absolutely, her cousin Woof. Another Bichon. She was a featured canine actress on the Parisian stage. Quite talented. She is living in the Meadows for the time being. My understudy is an angel."

The Duchess was her impatient, imperious self. "Well. Are you going to recruit Sherlock Holmes or not."

The Baroness had to resist the urge to smack her in the mouth. Wouldn't do at all. Not heavenly behavior. 'Yes, Your Grace. I have a few items and errands to attend to and then my dog and I will flit down to Earth."

Penelope shouted, "Hip, Hip Hurray! Three cheers for Baroness Crestwell and Sherlock Holmes. All for one and one for all."

Juliet thought, "She's an impulsive one, isn't she. I wonder how she died. Did her husband kill her to shut her up? I could sympathize with him if he did."

The ethereal Countess and Viscountess joined in the noisemaking. The Duchess maintained her sour visage. Raymond conveniently disappeared. Pookie cocked her head and barked. She had to find Woof and tell her she was going on stage in her place. She was none too pleased. After all that rehearsal. Oh well, there was still a lot of time left in the afterlife. Off she ran to the Meadows. Juliet headed to the Guild's Paradise Theatre. Next stop after that: 221B Baker Street.

*****

Sherlock Holmes was in the middle of one of his noxious experiments. Watson seemed impervious to the smell. Mrs. Hudson was carrying out the breakfast dishes and wishing she could hold her nose. As she was descending the stairs, she almost dropped the crockery and silverware. There shimmering on the staircase was a phantom, actually two phantoms, she knew all too well.

"Hello, Martha. The bad penny and her furry farthing have returned."

"Lady Juliet, what a delight. Back to see Mr. Holmes again? He's here doing one of his nasty chemical trials. What a stench! Hello, Pookie. Aren't you the lovely girl. Let me put these dishes down and I'll announce you two."

"No need! We'll just flit in as usual and surprise them. I assume Watson is with him"

"Oh yes, deeply engaged in reading his paper. He's totally indifferent to Mr. Holmes' concoctions. I wish I was. If your sense of smell is active you may want to cover your nose. Poor Pookie will probably have a sneezing fit."

"No, we're not physical this time. We're just delivering a celestial request. It's not from the Almighty but a group of deceased

147

suffragists who are very much upset. I hope Holmes is in a good mood."

"It will depend on whether his experiment works. I'll be up to join you shortly after I take care of the breakfast things."

The two wraiths flitted up the stairs and through the door. Watson looked up from his reading and smiled. "Holmes, we have company."

"Not now, Watson. I think I'm about to successfully invent synthetic rubber."

"It certainly smells pungent. Hello, Lady Juliet. Hello, Pookie. You both look lovely as usual."

"Thank you, Doctor. Always such a considerate gentleman. On the other hand…"

Holmes looked up, "Oh, hello, Baroness. Back again. As usual, your timing is terrible."

"Thank you, Sherlock. As usual, most welcoming. When you're finished puttering about, I have a request."

"I'm quite busy. No time for new engagements, even for Heaven."

"This isn't for Heaven. It's for the Women's Suffragist Movement."

"I support the cause but I'm much too occupied to get actively involved. Ask Watson!"

"Even to save a woman from being undeservedly hanged?"

That got his attention.

"Ah, you're referring to Lady Dorothy Fletcher and the attempted Parliament bombing. "

She should have known he'd be aware of the situation. *"Yes, I have it from reliable witnesses that she is innocent and being framed by an anonymous informant."*

"Who are these witnesses?"

"Well, not exactly witnesses. Deceased noblewomen who are strong supporters of the suffrage movement."

"Let me guess. They are led by Letitia Forsythe, former Duchess of Ailesworth, a women who collects causes like bees collect nectar. Only she seldom produces honey. My dear Baroness, the woman is a rabble rouser."

Juliet retorted. *"That may be but Lady Dorothy is confined in Holloway and due to be prosecuted for treason and attempted insurrection. Unlike the Windsor Castle incident, the explosion never took place. It's not even certain it was intended to. The three men involved vehemently deny any intent to bomb Parliament. Lady Dorothy says she doesn't even know who they are. Her first husband was a Fenian but he's long dead and she has had no Irish involvement since. Her current husband is Lord Fletcher, one of the few Marquesses in the realm. She is a Marchioness."*

"But she has been active with the Women's Social and Political Union (WSPU)."

"Oh yes, like many women, she marched, helped prepare materials and otherwise was a good soldier but hardly a plotter or assassin. I'm amazed Scotland Yard and the Home Office are taking the word of an anonymous informant."

"If I told you Athelney Jones is handling the case, would that explain it."

"Oh no! That idiot. He'll believe anything. He hates women. Remember how he treated the Salvation Army Major (Book One – A Major Issue) He never did apologize even after he was proven wrong. He would have seen her hung."

Watson, who had been listening intently to the conversation, exclaimed, "I say, Holmes, if anyone can cock up an investigation, it's Inspector Athelney Jones. I agree with Baroness Juliet. The man is an idiotic incompetent. How they let him stay on at the Yard is beyond me."

"His wrongheaded colleagues cover for him. Well, Milady, I was prepared to turn you down but since Jones is involved, there is a serious chance that justice is being miscarried once again. You can tell your clamorous ghosts that I will look into it. I'll talk to the lady and hear her story."

"Thank you. Pookie and I will keep you company."

"I suspected as much. Watson, what's your pleasure?"

"Anything to sink Athelney Jones."

While this discussion was going on, Mrs. Hudson had entered the room. Of course, she was aware of the Baroness and her dog ever since the adventure of the Girls' Night Out. "Are you going to vindicate that poor woman? Oh, I hope so, Mr. Holmes. Someone is trying to use her and get her hung. It's a disgrace. Count on you to do the right thing."

Sherlock Holmes knew when he had been outplayed. "I'll contact the governor of Holloway Prison and get him to agree to my seeing the lady. He's an old friend. We also need to contact her legal representative and her husband the Marquess. As the wife of a peer the Marchioness is entitled to be tried by the House of Lords but I'm not sure that's going to help her when she is accused of trying to blow up Parliament. Their lordships probably would not take kindly to attempted assassinations. All right, ladies, and you too Watson. I shall take on Lady Fletcher's case. You may inform the Duchess and her entourage."

Pookie barked and attempted to lick Holmes' face. "I am surrounded by ghostly females. With all due respect, Mrs. Hudson."

"No umbrage taken, Mr. Holmes. We ladies may not all have the vote yet but we do have influence."

Holmes smiled, shook his head and muttered. "Indeed!"

*****

Never one to miss an opportunity to take advantage of London's attractions, that evening Juliet took Pookie for an invisible tour of the shops and British subsidiaries and affiliates of the Parisian fashion houses. Edwardian styles were just surfacing and the French modistes were quick to take the lead in developing a "1903 look."

"Pookie, we'll have to convince Holmes and Raymond that a trip to Paris is required for this exercise to be a success. Ooh, look at those fabulous hats. I'd look divine in several of those creations although an ornate halo is actually divine enough. I must confer once again with the ethereal modistes of Miraculous Modes and tell them what I've seen. Madame Clarice is a genius. She can take heavenly cloth and mold it into such delicious confections. Actually, the London and Paris houses are well behind her in taste matched with boldness."

"Why don't we see if there is anything worth watching in the theatres. Last time we were here, that production of 'Where's Jane?' at the Palladium was a horror. Not at all the same show I starred in. I felt so sorry for Mrs. Hudson. She was looking forward

151

to a splendid Girls' Night Out. Little did I know that my ex-husband was going to meet his fate at that theatre. Oh well, it wasn't a complete loss. Dinner at Simpson's was spectacular. Let's see. Here's one show, a revue: 'Mystical Magical Mayhem.' Let's give that a try."

The Bichon looked skeptical. Ghosts knew all about mystical magic and dogs were great at mayhem. This sounded like a real stinker but who was she to argue with her mistress. Pookie had become a theatre critic ever since she got a part as the Celestial Canine in The Heavenly Theatre Guild's latest production. A real diva. She wanted to get back to Paradise before her understudy cousin Woof took over the role. Oh well, at least she could probably earn a Heavenly Chewy before the night is over.

*****

Closing down his successful experiments in synthetic rubber, Holmes and Watson were busy making appointments with The Marquess, Lord Fletcher; Mr. Amos Quiver Esq, solicitor to their Lordship and Ladyship and the Governor of Holloway Prison, Roger Mason. No doubt they would be hearing shortly from Athelney Jones as soon as he heard of Holmes' involvement.

His Lordship was most pleased that Holmes was engaging himself in the case and called on their solicitor to join in a strategy session with the detectives and himself the next morning at his town house. Warden Mason, who felt that Lady Dorothy was in his care courtesy of the idiot Inspector Jones, was only too willing to grant Holmes access to her. Unfortunately, he was obliged to inform Athelney Jones.

Needless to say, after observing another night of disappointing thespianism, Baroness Juliet and her furry companion were on hand for these meetings, roundly jeering and attempting to bite at Jones when and if he appeared. A shame he couldn't hear her or feel the dog's ethereal teeth.

The House of Lords was sitting that week so the Marquess had taken up residence in his London domicile near Hyde Park. A stately pile befitting the rank and privilege of Lord Fletcher, it loomed over the surrounding landscape not far from the Speakers' Corner and Grand Entrance.

Holmes and Watson presented their cards to the butler and followed him through an immense foyer decorated with the compulsory frowning portraits of noble ancestors. Juliet frowned back and Pookie whined. *"I never had my portrait painted, Pookie. Reginald was such a cheapskate. I would have smiled for the artist. It would have made a sharp contrast to the rest of the sourpusses cluttering up our walls. Now that Reginald has passed on, I'm not sure who inherits the house. Luckily, I won't have to put up with him in Heaven. Poor Reginald. He never liked heat. Oh, here we are. Can a mere Baroness look on a Marquess? Well, a cat can look at a queen. I'm sure the Duchess and her clamorous claque would be impressed."*

"My Lord, Mr. Sherlock Holmes and Doctor Watson are here as you requested."

The Marquess, in his early 50's, was an impressive individual. Tall, mustachioed, with shots of grey in his brown hair, impeccably tailored, he smiled graciously. "Gentlemen, welcome. Thank you for engaging yourselves on poor Dorothy's and my behalf. I am delighted to have your assistance. You will be amply compensated. Let me introduce my excellent solicitor, Mr. Amos Quiver, Esq."

The lawyer was unusually young to inspire the trust of the nobleman. Shorter than the Marquess *(and Holmes and Watson, for that matter)* and somewhat more carelessly dressed, his piercing blue eyes peered out from behind a pair of gold rimmed spectacles. His black hair and mutton chop whiskers lent an air of maturity but it was apparent that he had yet to see the far side of thirty. He extended his hand to the two detectives and said in a voice deeper than expected, "Gentlemen, I, too, welcome your support. Lady Dorothy is the victim of the worst sort of pernicious scheming exacerbated by the total lack of competence and stupidity of Scotland Yard. Unfortunately, because of the serious nature of the accusations against her, I have been unable to secure bail for her. This is one of those circumstances where the peer's privilege to be tried by the House of Lords may work to her detriment."

Watson shook his head. "We are all too familiar with the inept Inspector Athelney Jones."

Juliet chortled. Pookie growled.

Holmes intervened, "We understand, Mr. Quiver. Plotting against Parliament is not a crime their lordships are bound to countenance gently."

The Marquess spoke up. "But she did no such thing. In fact, I seriously doubt there was a plot at all. The three men insist they are innocent and don't even know Lady Dorothy."

The lawyer said, "They have been remanded to Newgate and their circumstances are hardly pleasant. The Warden at Holloway Prison for Women has been most gracious in accommodating Lady Dorothy's needs and comfort but of course, we must extricate her as soon as possible."

Holmes nodded, "It's my intention to track down this mysterious informant and put paid to his or her testimony. I am not the least bit surprised that Jones, a consummate misogynist, has fallen for the story. He has a fierce animosity for Suffragists. I doubt

154

if he even cares if the Fenians are involved. If a crime has been committed at all, we must ferret out the informant and convince Jones' superiors that once again he has been duped. Mr. Quiver, have you approached the Commissioner?"

"I have but he is reluctant to override the Inspector without countervailing evidence."

Watson snorted, "Well, we shall find the evidence for him. Is there a date set for her Ladyship's trial?"

"No, there is the complication of her being tried by the Lords while the three male plotters are to be brought before the central criminal court at the Old Bailey. There is a debate among the justices as to how to synchronize the presentation of evidence and witnesses and the conduct of the trial or trials."

The Marquess roared. "There is no evidence. No witnesses! Just the word of an anonymous informant. She is being tried in the press by a bunch of anti-nobility hacks."

"No doubt, your Lordship. I share your outrage on behalf of your wife, but we also owe it to the three accused men to secure their freedom if they are indeed innocent. I hope to be able to destroy this whole house of cards posing as testimony and demolish the need for any trial at all. First we must find this elusive informant. Mr. Quiver, what can you tell us? I assume as counsel for the defense, you have been presented with the so-called evidence."

"I have gotten precious little from Jones. An anonymous note addressed to the police. He has nothing else but he believes he has enough to remand her. He claims the threat against Parliament is too great to be ignored. I have entered a writ of habeas corpus but it is not clear whether the writ will apply in a case of peer privilege. Normally a peer can invoke freedom from arrest but treason and sedition are two of the few crimes that are exceptions. Lady Dorothy has been formally accused of treason."

"However, I am prepared to go back to the Commissioner. My client has a right to identify and face her accusers. I am not sure who is acting to defend the three men but they are entitled to the same consideration. I will endeavor to find out the identity of the solicitor or solicitors representing them. We cannot allow such flimsy and unsupported allegations to stand."

"We shall jointly beard Athelney Jones in his den. An unpleasant but necessary step."

The Marquess thanked them both. "I stand ready to assist in any way I can. My wife is innocent."

Lady Juliet was seething. *"That imbecile Jones probably sees this as a major career enhancer. His opportunity to make Chief Inspector on the backs of poor innocents. I wouldn't put it past him if he invented the anonymous informant and the letter himself. The man is incorrigible to say nothing of being a biased misogynist and dishonest to boot. Let's tear him apart, Holmes. I realize I'm not behaving in a saintly way and will probably be chastised for my attitude but he makes me so angry."*

Holmes responded telepathically, "Patience, Milady. There is more to this than Athelney Jones' stupidity and ambition. There may well be a plot but of a different type. I suspect the Marquess may be the true target. He has been a supporter of many causes unpopular with the privileged elite. His wife's disgrace could create an irreparable scandal in the House of Lords. He could even be impeached. His support of Women's Suffrage along with Irish Home Rule has caused an uproar in hostile circles. There are influential individuals behind this. We need to dig deeper than Inspector Jones but first we have to get the lady and the three men released while we investigate. Watson and I will join Mr. Quiver in his efforts."

"Don't forget Pookie and me!

"How could I possibly do that?"

"While you, Watson and Mr. Quiver are visiting the Marchioness and having at Athelney Jones, I will return to Heaven and further interview the Duchess and her boisterous companions. I'm sure they know more than they are telling. Come Pookie. Short trip back to Paradise and then we return to London." They flitted.

Holmes turned to the Marquess. "My Lord. I have a strong suspicion that this whole affair is being engineered to bring you down. Your wife is a surrogate victim as are the three so-called plotters. You have taken a number of unpopular stands in Parliament and created strong reactions among some of your peers. This may be their way of destroying your reputation along with Lady Fletcher's. Are you prepared to do battle, if necessary?"

"No one has ever accused a Fletcher of running from a fight. I have enemies. Any Member of Parliament who is worth his salt is going to have opponents. I have been outspoken in support of Women's Suffrage, partially due to Lady Dorothy's influence, I will admit. I am also an advocate for Irish Home Rule. Those two issues are bound to stir up controversy but this plot against my wife and those three men is a dastardly show of cowardice and depravity. And that fatuous idiot Jones is playing right into their hands."

"Who is 'they', Milord?"

"The Fundamentalist League - a group of peers, MPs, public officials, clergy and influentials whose avowed purpose in life is to preserve long standing English conventions and principles and subvert any attempts at progress and change. They are headed up by a Council. Their current leader is Lord Conroy, the Duke of Wessex. He is a crusty exemplar of the Old School but I don't believe he would stoop to a scandalous act such as this."

"He might not. But some firebrand members of the governing Council may have no such qualms. It may also be that some of them have mesmerized the ambitious Athelney Jones with promises of advancement if he abets their schemes. I would not put it past him but Watson, Mr. Quiver and I shall soon see. Jones is a notoriously poor liar. He has absolutely no skills at covering up duplicity. I think we can trap him into making admissions. We also need the names of the League's Council leaders."

The noble smiled. "That's easily done. They are in the press just about every day and making public pronouncements attacking progressives as undermining good old British Standards and Values. I'll get you a list."

Holmes turned to Watson and the lawyer. "Gentlemen, shall we see the Marchioness and then confront Inspector Jones?"

Watson groaned, "I think I'd rather have a tooth pulled."

Quiver laughed, "I haven't had my exercise with him today. Time for another round. But first, on to her Ladyship."

*****

The Governor of Holloway Prison, Roger Mason, greeted the three men. "Gentlemen. I'm delighted you're taking up the lady's cause. If ever I have met an innocent victim. it is she. I'm trying to make her as comfortable as prison life will allow. I doubt my colleagues at Newgate are extending the same hospitality to their three Irish inmates. Come with me and I'll introduce you."

He summoned a matron. "Miss Catherine. These gentlemen are here to speak with Marchioness Fletcher. Mr. Sherlock Holmes, Doctor John Watson and Mr. Amos Quiver, Esq."

"Oh, the poor lady. I'm glad to see she is finally getting some expert help. Don't expect much information from her. She is as confused as we all are. She claims she does not know any of the men involved and is completely in the dark as far as bombing Parliament is concerned. Here is her cell. Lady Fletcher, you have guests." She opened the cell door.

The Governor introduced the three of them. The Marchioness had clearly been crying and continuously twisted her hands in despair as she spoke. Slender to the point of emaciation, her dark hair uncombed, she sat on her bed and spoke in a barely audible whisper.

"Thank you for coming, gentlemen. My husband, the Marquess has been my only visitor. I guess I am being shunned by society, including my so-called friends from the Suffragist movement."

Holmes, aware of the Clamorous Ghosts who had recruited Lady Juliet, assured her that she had more friends working for her than she imagined.

"Thank you, Mr. Holmes. That is good to know. " *(Little did she realize that her allies were mostly ghosts, dead but hyperactive.)* I don't know what to tell you. Not only am I innocent. I am totally uninformed. I don't know who the three Irish men are. I have had no contact with them. Are they guilty of trying to bomb Parliament?"

"We believe not, milady. We believe this anonymous letter implicating the four of you is a pernicious fraud unfortunately accepted by a biased and stupid Scotland Yard Inspector. He is our next stop."

"I have no knowledge of how to construct, deliver or detonate a bomb of any sort least of all one that would destroy Parliament. Oh. I am so confused. I am frantic."

The Governor smiled, "Fear not, milady. If I were in desperate straits, these are exactly the individuals I would want in my corner."

Watson smiled. "We will expend all our efforts on your behalf, milady. We hope to have you out of here in record time."

"Thank you Doctor. But what of my reputation and my husband's? We will be pariahs by the time the press gets finished with us."

Quiver shook his head. "Someone will be a pariah but it will not be you or the Marquess. Courage milady. Just a little longer."

*****

"No, Pookie. We don't have time for you to join your canine friends for a game of fetch. I have an appointment with - Letitia Forsythe, former Duchess of Ailesworth, Lady Agnes Faulkner, former Countess of Durham; Viscountess Sarah Wellington and Miss Penelope Swift - the Clamorous Ghosts -and then we have to flit back to London."

This time the ghostly meeting took place at the Duchess' celestial villa. Not much different from the home of the Baroness. Heaven was a great leveler. She took some exception to the dog being present but backed down when she recalled Lady Juliet was working for the Marchioness on her behalf as well as her fellow deceased aristocrats.

"Baroness, do you have any news for us? Oh, I do hope so." Penelope Swift was being her usual hyper energetic self.

"Mr. Holmes has taken on the assignment, has met with Lady Fletcher's solicitor and is engaged right now with the Marquess. He is meeting Lady Fletcher and then his next stop is the Scotland Yard Inspector who has used the anonymous note of accusation to imprison the Marchioness. However, ladies, I have the feeling that you have not been totally forthcoming with what you know or suspect about this whole affair."

The Countess and Viscountess stared at the ceiling while Penelope blanched. The Duchess loudly cleared her throat. "I don't know what you mean, Lady Juliet."

"I mean, I believe that you have strong suspicions who is behind this fraud but are witholding that information. I believe that you are invoking Sherlock Holmes' good offices in the hope that he will solve the problem without revealing the true culprits. I'm sorry but that's not the way Mr. Holmes works. He won't be satisfied until he brings the villain or villains to book."

She continued, "Now, who are you protecting? Your consciences are bothering you because the Marchioness and the three men are imprisoned as a result of the activities of someone you all know. Someone you are reluctant to reveal. Ladies! Either you give me the names or I will return to Earth and most regretfully tell Holmes and Watson to abandon the case. Lady Dorothy will have to rely on her solicitor's efforts."

As expected, it was Penelope who crumpled. "Oh, Tell her, My Lady. Tell her!"

The Duchess sighed, "It's my son, Arthur. The Duke's Heir Presumptive. He is an agitator and firmly committed to defeat Women's Suffrage. He's also against child and worker relief. He

161

wants to eliminate all Irish attempts at self government. He has led resistance to tax increases. We had endless battles before I passed on. My husband, the Duke, supports Suffrage and Home Rule and Arthur and he are estranged as a result. Arthur is a member of The Fundamentalist League Ruling Council. Actually he leads it. Lord Conroy, the Duke of Wessex is the chairman but he's just a figurehead. I believe Arthur's behind this anonymous letter accusing Lady Fletcher and the men. But after all is said and done, he is my son. I just want Holmes to undo what damage he has caused and set things to right."

The Baroness responded. 'I'm not sure Holmes can set things to right. That's your son's responsibility but it doesn't sound like he might be willing to do so. I'm afraid he's gone too far."

"Well, what about this Inspector Jones, Can't Holmes get him to cancel his arrests?"

"I'm sure Holmes intends to try but I'm not hopeful. Athelney Jones is a thick headed fool. Just the type your son can bully and cajole into doing his will. We've had dealings with him before. Do you have anything else you wish to tell me? I'm due back in London. No? Come Pookie, we have to flit."

Penelope was wringing her hands and sobbing. The Countess and Viscountess just stared at her and the Duchess. Oh dear! This sort of thing was not supposed to happen in Paradise.

*****

As the trio was about to leave Holloway Prison for Scotland Yard, the Baroness flitted up to Holmes. She could be seen and heard by the Great Detective and Watson but of course, Mr. Quiver was unaware of her existence. To say nothing of the dog. Watson took things in hand and suggested that they stop for lunch before going on to deal with Athelney Jones. Holmes took the hint and said he had a short errand to run but would join them at the Criterion. The doctor and lawyer hailed a cab and off they went leaving Holmes behind.

Juliet huffed, *"Well, you've led Pookie and me a merry chase. Mrs. Hudson told me where to find you. I have news."*

She repeated almost verbatim her conversation with the Duchess and her retinue.

Holmes mused, "So, the evil genius behind this scheme is Sir Arthur Ailesworth, the presumptive successor to the Duke. Let us place his Lordship on our visitation list. If, as you say, he and his son are estranged, he may be willing to assist in upsetting this plot once we have proven it. I didn't think Jones had the audacity or imagination to think it up by himself. It's imperative we trace that letter from the so-called anonymous informant. It has to exist. Jones needed to show it to the commissioner and the magistrates in order to facilitate the arrests. I doubt he still has it in his possession. I'll leave it to Mr. Quiver to secure it as trial evidence. I think both the Duke and the Marquess can apply sufficient pressure to assist the solicitor."

"Let's hope there is no need for a trial. The Duchess wants her son to get off with a wrist slap. He's vicious and arrogant. After what he's done, he should spend time in gaol. He's not entitled to peer privilege."

"Let's not get ahead of ourselves, Baroness. I tend to agree with you but there is the small matter of proving an influential like Sir Arthur is at the bottom of this. We may have the Duke and the Marquess but The Fundamentalist League and its Ruling Council also has some powerful members. We have to hope a sufficient number of them will be disgusted when faced with sufficient evidence and move to expel the culprit. Then Mr. Quiver can pursue

163

a lawsuit for conspiracy and false arrest. If it turns out he was aware of and complicit with the chicanery involved, we may be able to break Athelney Jones in the process."

"That's too much to hope for, Holmes. Perhaps we can get Pookie and her canine friends to materialize yet again and bite him to death." (She giggled.)

"Perhaps not the canine cadre but my other associates, The Irregulars. Harassing the police is one of their specialties."

"Those urchins fascinate me. I've only met them briefly. I want to get to know them better." (Little did she know.) *"I'll brief Watson later on my session with the ghosts. Martha Hudson is curious. Should I inform her?"*

"Why not! She may be helpful. Well, there's no putting it off further. But I'll eschew lunch in favor of a stop at the St. James Club and Langdale Pike. You have no need of food but perhaps you might give your dog one of those Heavenly Chewies." Pookie perked up, panted and whined. The Baroness reached into her infinite reticule and pulled out a treat.

"Who or what is Langdale Pike?"

"The wholesale purveyor and collector of London's gossip. If anyone has information on Sir Arthur Ailesworth, Pike is our man. He sits in the bow window of his club, apprently immobile and inert and yet he has his antennae sharply tuned for the latest disgraces, rumors, tittle-tattle and outrages. He filters these and passes them on to the press and chattering classes, all for a price of course."

"He's reminiscent of your brother."

"Mycroft may be indolent but he is not inactive. He certainly is all-knowing and responsible. And he despises Fleet Street and the scandal mongers."

"I stand corrected. I'm eager to meet this gentleman. I assume he is a gentleman."

"Watson doesn't think so. The good Doctor despairs of my associating with Pike. He believes he is a disreputable cad. It may be true, I suppose, but Pike is also quite useful to a Consulting Detective such as myself. His information is usually quite reliable and I supply him with occasional fodder to supplement his insatiable appetite. It's just as well that Watson is off having lunch with Mr. Quiver, an honorable member of the legal profession. I'm sure I shall hear protests from him. However, for the nonce, on to St. James."

As Sherlock Holmes descended from his cab at the St. James Club, Langdale Pike spied him from his bow window perch. His interest was immediately piqued. Holmes never approached the club unless he had some reason to deal with Pike. He was unaware of the two phantoms accompanying the detective. Their interest in him was also immediately aroused.

He waved an indolent hand in Holmes direction and drawled. "Mr. Sherlock Holmes. Always a pleasure. Are you buying or selling?"

"A bit of both, Langdale. Perhaps a swap may be in order."

"Ooh, interesting. Please have a seat. We can speak confidentially here. Perhaps a bit of liquid refreshment to facilitate the discussion?"

"Thank you, no, but don't let me stop you."

"I'll abstain. The club's alcohol resources have fallen on hard times of late. If it were not for this ideal view of London's passing parade, I might consider a change of venue. But I digress. Who or what is our topic du jour?"

"Sir Arthur Ailesworth!"

"I congratulate you, Mr. Holmes. You always succeed in producing juicy subjects. In what way are you involved with the fearsome Sir Arthur? He is awash in issues and enemies."

"Lady Dorothy Fletcher!"

"Ah, the imprisoned Marchioness. You believe Sir Arthur is somehow responsible for her unfortunate circumstances? Let us not forget the Irishmen ensconced in Newgate, as well."

"I have very strong suspicions and am currently in search of unimpeachable truth. Speaking of impeachment, I think the Marquess is the real target of Sir Arthur's chicanery. The disgrace of a wife convicted of treason by no less than the House of Lords would be too much for him to withstand. He would have to resign from Parliament and withdraw from society, perhaps even leave the country."

Pike frowned, "I share your suspicions. This anonymous letter that has Scotland Yard all atwitter probably came from him. Certain members of The Fundamentalist League are upset by his overweening attempts to control the Council and unseat the chairman, Lord Conroy, the Duke of Wessex. Conroy is a figurehead but he has a number of old school chums, acquaintances and political suitors in his capacious pocket. Sir Arthur has a tough row to hoe. Taking on the Marquess will be no easy task. He also has to contend with his father, the Duke, who opposes Arthur at probably every turn."

"Of course, our young firebrand is not without his own supporters. But I think I know one or another of his clique who can be convinced that they are in peril of being exposed for this conspiracy if they continue to back Sir Arthur. Let me do a bit of digging, my specialty. I'll have a witness for you by tomorrow evening. What a splendid set of headlines exposing the presumptive Duke will make. Presumptive, ha! Presumptuous is more like it. If I succeed, we will have to negotiate a fair exchange, Mr. Sherlock Holmes."

Holmes smiled, "I will have my rogue and you will have your story. Sounds fair to me, Langdale. However, perhaps a bottle of Grand Champagne Cognac to offset the deteriorating St. James Club cellar."

Pike smiled back. "Two bottles!"

Lady Juliet had been listening to this dialogue. As they left the club, she whistled a merry little tune and Pookie rotated on her hind legs.

"Well, that was entertaining. Is he really as good as all that?"

"His record is quite impressive. I can't guarantee he'll succeed but I have high expectations. I'll have to make an appointment with His Grace Lord Ailesworth to discuss his son. But now let's stop at the Criterion and collect Watson and Mr. Quiver and then on to Scotland Yard and Inspector Jones."

*****

Athelney Jones stretched back in his office chair, unaware that serious changes were about to impinge on his professional career and indeed, his life. He felt smug. His arrest of Marchioness Fletcher and those three Irish insurrectionists was working out just the way Sir Arthur had predicted. Soon he would be 'Chief' Inspector Jones! It had a nice ring to it.

The start of the criminal hearings was taking longer than he had hoped but the situation was complicated by the lady's peer privilege. It wasn't often, if ever, that the wife of a Marquess was subjected to trial procedures, especially for treason. On top of that, the evidence, the anonymous letter from an equally anonymous "informant" also applied to the three Irishmen who swore they weren't Fenians. Liars! Lawyers were fighting over access to the letter. It was locked away in the Desk of the Lord High Steward pending submission to the courts in question - The House of Lords and the Old Bailey.

The door to his office opened and a constable popped his head in. "Excuse me, Inspector but you have visitors and they won't take 'no' for an answer."

"Who..." He stopped as Sherlock Holmes appeared in the doorway. That pest Doctor Watson was with him and that damn lawyer, Quiver.

Lady Juliet and Pookie flitted past him but occupied no space at all in the modest office. The three men entered without being admitted and squeezed around the desk.

"What's the meaning of this, Sherlock Holmes? And you. Mr. Quiver! Why are you back? I told you that the letter is no longer in my hands. The charges against Lady Fletcher are significant and I was justified in having her arrested and confined. I have nothing else to say."

Holmes stared at Jones. "We didn't come here to listen to you, Inspector but to tell you, nay, warn you. You are backing the wrong horse. His days of influence are numbered. We are about to topple him and you with him."

168

"That's where you're wrong, Holmes. Sir Arthur Ailesworth is a formidable individual and a fearsome enemy."

Juliet grinned, *"Stupid as usual! Oh Jones, you just admitted to being in thrall to the presumptive heir to the Ailesworth dukedom. You are such an ass."*

Holmes looked at the Inspector. "So you acknowledge your relationship to Sir Arthur. I assume he is your anonymous but reliable informant and engineered this whole calamity."

Athelney Jones was clearly rattled. "Now wait a minute. I did no such thing. I don't even know this Sir Arthur. Who is he?"

"Then how do you know he is a formidable individual and a fearsome enemy? You are an inept liar, Inspector. I think the Commissioner will be interested. Shall we meet with him?"

"Hold on. No need to call the Commissioner's attention to such a trivial matter."

Watson exploded, "You call condemning four people to potential hanging for treason a trivial matter! You'll be lucky if you're not indicted for false arrest and conspiracy. You're a disgrace to Scotland Yard and the Empire. Fleet Street will have a festival. We'll see to it that you are back walking a beat, ex-Inspector, or arrested and out of the job completely."

Juliet chortled and Pookie barked, *"Give it to him, Watson. Scare him to death. On second thought, No! I wouldn't want to see him as a ghost. Even a ghost on his way to Hell."*

Holmes stared banefully. "What's it to be, Jones? Running to your protector and co-conspirator will do you no good. He'll leave you swinging in the wind. A confession will probably get you off more lightly. Isn't that what you always say to the criminals you arrest? Who wrote the letter, Inspector? You or Sir Arthur? Mr.

169

Quiver is our star witness. Can you recover the letter from the Lord High Steward, Mr. Quiver?"

"As evidence of the Inspector's malfeasance, I believe so, Mr. Holmes."

"Splendid! I believe the Commissioner is in his office. Shall we go?"

*****

"So, Mr. Holmes, you believe my son conspired to have the Marchioness and those three Irish unfortunates accused of treason and incarcerated in order to bring down Marquess Fletcher."

"Yes, your Grace. I do. Sir Arthur has both extreme ambitions and strong traditionalist beliefs. He has no scruples when it comes to promoting his wishes. I am sorry to say, this conspiracy demonstrates his total lack of values and disregard for decency or the welfare of others. I plan to approach Lord Conroy, the Chair of the Fundamentalist League and seek to have your son expelled. The Commissioner of Scotland Yard is seeking further evidence of collusion with the Inspector who arrested the Marchioness and the non-Fenians. Mr. Quiver, the solicitor to Lord and Lady Fletcher is even now managing her release from Holloway and the freedom of the men at Newgate. The Lord High Steward of the House of Lords has quashed the accusations and altered the investigations into scrutiny of Sir Arthur's activities."

"Well, Mr. Holmes, if what you say is true and it turns out Arthur is guilty, he can expect to be fully disowned. Our relationship has been rocky to say the least but this takes the biscuit. I shall speak to the Home Secretary and Lord Conroy. If you uncover any further evidence to prove his guilt, I would be obliged to hear it. Thank you."

*****

Langdale Pike once again spied the Consulting Detective approaching the St. James Club. He noticed he was carrying two bottles of what Pike hoped was vintage cognac. He, in turn, had further evidence which Sherlock Holmes could use in his campaign against Sir Arthur Ailesworth. The detective joined him, extending his alcoholic gifts and said, "Your information on the Fundametalist League and Sir Arthur's influence in it was most helpful. He is on his way out the door as we speak."

"Lord Conroy woke up from his torpor sufficiently to express his outrage at the conspiracy against the Marquess and Marchioness Fletcher and to incite enough members of the League to vote Sir Arthur out. I am now searching for enough proof to have him indicted for conspiring to suborn justice resulting in false arrest. Athelney Jones has characterized himself as a deceived victim of the duplicitous nobleman. The Commissioner has supended judgement on the matter but I would not want to wager on the Inspector's fate. Needless to say, all charges against all imprisoned parties have been dropped and they have been released. Do you have anything more to share?"

"Ah, yes indeed! It seems our friend has a long and chequered history. Assault on a social scientist. Driving a horse drawn wagon into a parade of Suffragists. Engineering a major brawl on St. Patrick's Day. Setting fires to soup kitchens. Substantial injuries in every case. Fortunately, no deaths. None of these done personally, of course. He has a team of bully boys he employs to do his dirty work. This attack on the Marchioness is a step up the social ladder. First time he was directly involved although he's left that Scotland Yard jackass to take the blame."

"Can we prove any of these incidents are his doing?"

171

"Until recently, no, but it seems the noble's father has cut him off without a penny which left him to do his own mischief. He owes his gang monies for services rendered and several of them are willing to blow the whistle on him and supply proof provided they are paid and held blameless."

"It goes against my principles but I want to put an end to this scourge. I'm confdent the Marquess and Sir Arthur's father will both be willing to cooperate. I shall speak to both of them as well as the Scotland Yard Commissioner yet again. Many thanks, Langdale. I believe another two bottles of cognac are called for."

"Bless you, my son. I will make contact with the disgruntled minions. You will have your evidence."

*****

The Marchioness sailed into her drawing room and smiled. Looking a bit drawn from her experience in durance vile, she said, "I understand I have you, Mr. Holmes, Doctor Watson and Mr. Quiver to thank for my release. I hope my husband has already shown his gratitude."

"We have been amply rewarded. Thank you, milady."

An invisible little white dog whined. *"Yes, Pookie. You'll be rewarded too when we return to Paradise. A bagful of Heavenly Chewies awaits. More fun at the Meadows. You can also reclaim your star turn in the Theatre Guild's Saintly Spectacular. Don't worry, we'll find another role for your understudy, Woof. She won't steal your thunder or be unemployed."*

Back at 221B Baker Street, Watson was recording the events of the past few days. "What do we know of Athelney Jones' future, Holmes?"

"Undetermined, Watson. I think the Commissioner is waiting for all of this to blow over and the Fleet Street jackals to

172

find new sources of scandal. He is not eager to air the Yard's dirty laundry but don't be surprised if you see Inspector Jones back in constable's brass and blues walking a beat in one of the seamier parts of town. Or perhaps as a commissionaire at one of the midrange hotels. Sir Arthur was intercepted leaving the country. His fate is in limbo. Certainly not Heaven, eh Baroness?"

Lady Juliet was engaged in girl talk with Martha Hudson. They had become fast friends. Martha, in spite of her aversion to animals had fallen in love with Pookie. The feelings were reciprocated.

"I shall exert some celestial charity, Holmes, and avoid condemning him. Heaven is finally rubbing off on me."

"I assume you owe a report to the Duchess and her coterie."

"Yes, Penelope Swift will be beside herself with excitement. I feel sorry for the Duchess having such a cad for a son. Oops, there goes the celestial charity. But she brought it to our attention. Oh well, time to flit back, Pookie. Thank you, Holmes, for taking up the cause of the Clamorous Ghosts. You, no doubt, will be blessed. Farewell Doctor. It was good seeing you again. Goodbye Martha. Till we next meet." They disappeared.

Mrs. Hudson stared at the empty space. "Do you think they'll be back, Mr. Holmes?"

"I think you can count on it, Mrs. Hudson, Scarlet gown, white fur, red bow, haloes and all!"

Irregularities

"All right, Pookie. After our drills in formation flying with the True Angels, we deserve some time off. I must say I admire your aerial control. The squadron leader was much impressed."

The Bichon flew a short victory lap and landed next to Baroness Crestwell, Lady Juliet Armstrong. "Decked out in our scarlet flight suits, the two of us present a fetching image, don't we? Speaking of fetching, what say we flit over to the Meadows? I'm sure there's a game of multi-dimensional fetch going on in the canine zone. You always enjoy that although I haven't a clue what the contest rules are. I have a question for Mr. Sherman so we both can be busy."

They flitted out the door of the mansion, past the Elysian Fields, down to the Pearly Gates and the entry desk, a wave to St Peter, over the Rainbow Bridge and on to the Meadows. Pookie peeled off and joined the barking, whining and panting group as the game went into overtime, tied at three thousand and six. Time out! Toby was officiating, Celeste was scorekeeper and as usual, Marshall was protesting. Cinco was arguing with Toby in Spanish. Coach Tinker welcomed Pookie to the fray as she substituted for the pooped out Ms. Woof. Penny Lane led a series of cheers and the water bowls were miraculously filled automatically and not so miraculously emptied by the players. Juliet shrugged and turned toward the cloud covered administration building where Mr. Sherman and his team held sway.

The doors swung open and the former naturalist, now dirctor of the vast Meadows expanse, emerged alone. Mr. Sherman (Juliet never learned his first name) smiled and waved at the Baroness. "Lady Juliet, welcome. As you can see, I'm alone. My team is scattered about tending to their charges. Can I do something for you or are you here to simply relax? Heaven can sometimes be a bit of a trial."

Little did he know about Juliet's recent adventure in London with Sherlock Holmes trying to prevent a noblewoman's trial for treason.

"Actually, Mr. Sherman. There is something. You can tell me about Sherlock Holmes' group of street urchins, The Baker Street Irregulars. I understand you and Toby were great friends of theirs."

"Ah yes! A wonderful group of scruffy young lads. Actually there is a girl or two but they dress as boys. They loved Toby and Celeste. Helped me bury them when they died. What do want to know?

"Everything you can tell me!"

"Well, that's a pretty tall order. What is your interest?"

"Those children are living rough. Their lives are in danger. Holmes provides them with a small stipend but I doubt if they have any other source of income or any place to live that even comes close to a home. Pookie and I are living *(well, not really living)* here in splendor while they're in squalor. I want to help. I know there are many more in the same condition. I wish I had done more when I was still alive. So tell me about them. Then maybe I can persuade Holmes and Watson to help improve their conditions."

"Milady, you should realize that many of them choose to live the way they do rather than exist in a workhouse or some other dismal and oppressive place. Their options are extremely limited as they are for all the poor and illiterate. These children lack education. Many can't read or write but they are extremely clever. They often

175

outsmart criminals and law officers alike. But your charitable instincts do you credit. Let me think."

"How many Irregulars are there and how old are they?"

"The number varies but I should guess there's about six or seven of them. I remember Doctor Watson calling them 'half a dozen of the dirtiest and most ragged Street Arabs that ever I clapped eyes on.' Their ages are probably eight to twelve. They are distinguished by the fact that they are indistinguishable. No one notices them as they go about their business *(or Holmes' business)* of spying, delivering messages, finding individuals, places and situations. That's how they met Toby. Tracking down a villain."

"Are they organized?"

"Not entirely. They have a leader, Wiggins by name. He's somewhat older and extremely intelligent. He also can read and write and has some skills with numbers. Some of them have specialties. Causing disturbances, listening to conversations and reporting back, stealing, picking pockets."

"So they're little criminals."

"In a way. It's how they survive. Holmes pays them a shilling a day. Wiggins gets more. I'm not sure that they can hold on to the money. Some bully is always trying to take it away. They're not bad at fighting back, however. But when it comes to food, no fruit stand or costermonger is off limits. Holmes tries to wean them off picking pockets and often has them return their spoils to the owners. On the other hand, that's how they intercept some of the evidence he needs to bring a criminal to justice. It's a complicated relationship."

"What can I do?"

"Well, I know it's a temptation for a woman but you can avoid trying to clean up their appearance. First off, their raggedness is part of their talent and usefulness. Second, that's the condition they prefer. Some of them want to learn to read and write but they have an aversion to any kind of formal education. You won't get them to go to school if any institution would take them. Perhaps a tutor who is one of their own. I'd suggest you talk to Holmes although he may be sensitive to anyone interfering with his detective army. Watson may be a better choice. By now, I'm sure you are quite capable of managing both of those worthies. By the way, Mrs. Hudson is horrified by them although she is not above feeding them when they show up. As I say, it's complicated."

"Thank you, Mister Sherman. I'll heed your advice. Anything new in the Meadows?"

"Yes, we have our first unicorn."

"Really?"

"No, just joking! Oh, I think somebody just scored at the multi-dimensional fetch game breaking the tie. It may have been Pookie."

"Oh dear, I'll never get her to come home. And if she does, she'll be intolerable. The little egotist is a fur covered diva."

*****

"Mr. Holmes, that scruffy youngster, Wiggins, is here. He says it's important to talk to you. Should I let him up?"

"Yes, please, Mrs. Hudson. I have an assignment for him and his companions."

Sherlock Holmes was alone in his rooms at 221B Baker Street. Watson was out on a medical call. Mrs. Hudson stood aside

177

at the outer door and waved the Street Arab in. The sound of bounding feet echoed up the staircase and a thin teenager rushed through the open doorway to Holmes' apartment.

Eager for another fund of 'three and six', his pay and expenses for sleuthing on the detective's behalf, he whipped off his cap and breathlessly said, " 'Ere I am as ordered, Mister 'olmes. Whatcha?"

"A surveillance job for you and your associates, Wiggins. It will probably take all of you to keep tabs on Marty Clemson. He's back on the streets."

" 'E's a real piece of work! What's the bloke done this time?"

"He's been seen in and around Hatton Garden possibly casing several of the upscale jewelry stores. The police are on to him but as you know, he's a wily individual. Scotland Yard has asked me to join in a watch for him and his gang and in turn, I'm assigning you and rest of the Irregulars to scouting duty. Usual wages, report each morning or whenever you pick up something suspicious. Don't confront them but use the police whistles I've given you. The Met has assigned constables round the clock."

"We'll have to be sure the Peelers don't run us in!

"Some of the Bobbies know a few of you and you know them. I'll be on call and you'll all be accounted for. Do all of your partners know Clemson?"

"We know 'im. Not sure who he's pallin' around with, though. Time for a meetin'. We'll sort it out."

"Be careful. I don't want any of you hurt."

"You know us, Mr. "Olmes. We don't exist. We're ghosts."

178

The detective smiled and said, "Not quite! Not quite! I know a real one."

Wiggins stared at him.

*****

"Raymond, I need a favor." The Baroness had finally managed to separate Pookie from her doggie chums with a generous supply of Heavenly Chewies. The Bichon had indeed scored several times in the multi-dimensional fetching contest and her teammates had celebrated their victory in raucous canine style. The two of them returned to the baronial mansion and Pookie promptly plopped in her bed, exhausted but triumphal.

Lady Juliet had called on Mr. Raymond, a Senior Celestial Director, charged with keeping Paradise in heavenly shape. He also attempted, semi-successfully, to keep the Baroness and her dog under control. A middle-aged male, tall, dressed in morning *(mourning?)* clothes, clean shaven, not a hair out of place, dark eyes, color undetermined. As usual, he seemed to be floating inches above the ground.

"I anticipated your call, milady. Which one of you is in trouble this time?"

"Neither one of us, oddly enough. I want to perform a good deed."

She proceeded to tell him of her conversation with Mr. Sherman and described the Irregulars.

"We are aware of them, Baroness. Sherlock Holmes employs them quite frequently. We don't know how to categorize them. They pick pockets and steal food but it's for their survival and that of their families. On the other hand, they assist the detective in bringing rogues to justice. A strange combination. Like young

179

Robin Hoods. Irregulars is a most appropriate title for those urchins."

"I want to help them. Holmes keeps the wolf from their doors but they have no opportunities to really better themselves. I still remember living from hand to mouth as a chorus girl before I became a musical comedy star and then a Baroness. It wasn't as bad as these kids have it but it wasn't fun. Thank God I had an opportunity to get a modest education. That's what I want to do. I want to get them a modest education. Reading, writing, doing their sums."

"Milady, that's quite noble but I sincerely doubt you'll get them to go to school."

"That's what Mr. Sherman said. If I can't get them to school, I'll bring school to them. I'll convince Holmes and Watson to get them a tutor and pay them to take lessons. Wiggins can read and write. The rest of his crew should be able to as well."

"This tutor has to be one of their kind. No schoolmarm will do."

"I realize that. I know someone who could help. Remember Major Philomena Monahan of the Salvation Army. *(Book One – A Major Issue)* I'm sure she'll be more than willing to find the right person. I need to contact Holmes and Watson."

"So you and Pookie want to return to London."

"Have I ever told you that you are very insightful, Raymond."

"We Directors are immune from flattery, Baroness. This is Heaven after all."

"But you'll agree to our going back."

"I don't suppose I have a choice. However, your Bichon seems exhausted."

"Too much time in the Meadows playing multi-dimensional fetch. Those dogs are formidable."

"I'll clear your transit with the Pearly Gates archangels. No need to seek out St. Peter. Five days as usual. Holmes and Watson are your contacts. They can deal with Major Monahan or whomever."

"And Martha Hudson! We're good friends. She even likes Pookie."

"And Martha Hudson, poor soul" He disappeared

"Pookie, wake up, lazy bones."

At the word "bones" the Bichon opened her eyes, licked her chops and promptly fell back to sleep.

"Come on, girl. Let's go see Holmes, Watson and Mrs. Hudson. Did you lose your halo again? It's probably back at the Meadows. I don't know what to do with you." She snapped her fingers and a jaunty dog-sized corona appeared over the animal's head and a red bow wound around her neck. "There, that's better. You could use a bath but we'll let it pass. All right! Time to flit to London."

Juliet snapped her fingers again and changed into one of her traveling outfits – scarlet, of course. *(No, she was not a scarlet woman. In Heaven? Hardly!)*

Out the opaline doors, past the Elysian Fields, around the admissions desk and the Pearly Gates, over the Rainbow Bridge and down to London they flew. They arrived at Baker Street and 221B just in time to see Sherlock Holmes climb in a cab *(the third one)* and head out for parts unknown.

Juliet hoped Doctor Watson was on hand. She wanted to talk to him first. Actually, she wanted to say hello to Martha Hudson first.

The landlady was emerging from her rooms when she spotted the two wraiths coming through the door *(literally)*.

"Lady Juliet and Pookie. As I live and breathe."

"And we don't" Juliet giggled telepathically.

Martha blushed. "Oh dear, no, you don't. Do you? Anyway, I'm so glad to see you back. What brings you to Baker Street? Not another celestial crime, I hope."

"No! Nothing untoward this time. I have an idea I want to discuss with Holmes and Watson."

Pookie had put her paws up on Mrs. Hudson's leg. She was uncomfortable with dogs and other animals for that matter but was enchanted with the Bichon. She patted her ghostly head and ruffled her ears.

"Oh, I'm sorry. Mr. Holmes has just left. As usual, he didn't tell me where he was going or when he'd be back."

"That's fine. Is the good doctor here?"

"Yes, he just arrived back from making his rounds. Shall I announce you."

"No, don't bother yourself. Those stairs must be wearing on your mortal legs. We'll just flit up to their rooms. We'll stop by later to see you."

Up the staircase, through the door and into the center of the sitting room. Watson had just poured himself a measure of brandy and was about to settle into the basket chair with the day's newspaper when the two ghosts appeared. Wiping off the liquor that he had spilled on his waistcoat on their appearance, he smiled and said, "Baroness Juliet and Miss Pookie. How nice to see you again. You've just missed Holmes."

"That's all right, Doctor. I'm here to see both of you. I have a proposal having to do with the Baker Street Irregulars."

"Ah, the Street Arabs. Holmes' scruffy protégés. How can they help you when they can't see or hear you."

"No, I want to help them. But you're right. I need an intermediary or intermediaries."

"I assume I am being called on to fulfill that role."

"Got it in one, Doctor. You and Holmes and Major Monahan of the Salvation Army who can't see or hear me but somehow knows Pookie and I exist."

"Yes, I remember. She thanked Holmes and me for her deliverance and then thanked God and you. I've often wondered how she knew."

"She has very strong faith, doctor. As they say, It can move mountains."

He laughed, "Or conjure up spirits."

"I guess so."

"So what is this proposal about the Baker Street Irregulars?"

"They need to be educated. If Mr. Sherman is correct, Wiggins is the only one who can read, write and do sums. They

need to learn for their own good and safety. He mustn't be the only one."

"You're probably right but I doubt you'll be able to get the others into a schoolroom. They want nothing to do with education. You'll never get them before a teacher."

"They would if they were paid and had a tutor who was one of them. We need to convince Holmes. They'll do what he wants. I think Major Monahan can find someone who could teach them. I'm not being a do-gooder although that's the Heavenly way. They need more than their shilling and stolen fruit."

"All right. You convince Holmes and I'll speak to the Major."

*****

Atop the Hatton Garden Fine Jewelry Emporium, a pair of small, thin figures sat in the dark, watching two skylights. Simpson and Charlie, members of the Baker Street Irregulars for about two years, were on duty. Unnoticed, they had taken up their stations after being sent up there by Wiggins. Earlier, the leader of the Street Arabs had casually slipped along Holborn, Clerkenwell and Saffron Hill, tracking the movements of Marty Clemson as he seemingly wandered around the jewelry district.

Clemson had made several stops in front of the Emporium, the last time to meet another individual. They then slipped around a corner, vanished and reappeared a few minutes later climbing up and over the edges of the shop's roof and landing on the tiles. They stealthily approached one of the skylights only to be greeted by loud bursts of two police whistles. Clemson whipped around in the direction of the sounds and fired off a pistol, grazing Charlie's arm. They were immediately surrounded by several constables and dragged down to the ground level where they were taken into custody. Sherlock Holmes who had been waiting for the hidden urchins' signals sprinted up to the wounded youngster and proceeded to take him to the nearby Foundling Hospital.

The boy protested. "Ere Mr. Olmes. I ain't goin' to any charity Hospital and School. They'll never let me out. Can't Doctor Watson fix me up?"

Holmes ripped his shirt sleeve and fashioned a makeshift tourniquet, summoned a growler and rushed Charlie, Wiggins and Simpson back to Baker Street. Watson, Mrs. Hudson, the Baroness and Pookie were chatting in the sitting room when the foursome arrived. Watson immediately fell to and cleaned and bandaged the superficial wound. Mrs. Hudson rushed to her kitchen and returned with several meat pies which the boys gulped down. Wiggins then asked for their pay and over the protests of the adults, the urchins took the money and ran down the stairs and disappeared.

Juliet had told Martha Hudson of her intentions to get the Irregulars a basic education and she enthusiastically approved. The women had been haranguing Watson *(who had already agreed)* and then turned to Holmes and insisted he support the Baroness' plan. *"If those urchins are going to survive, they need to know how to read, write and do sums. Do you know how they handle the money you give them? Is some grifter cheating them? They can't go on forever as your secret army. You'll need new recruits."*

Holmes doubted he could get the Street Arabs to go along with the proposal but said he would try. But first they needed to contact Major Monahan. That was Watson's assignment. And Juliet's.

*****

Major Philomena Monahan rose from her desk in the offices of the London Salvation Army and extended her hand to Watson. The Baroness and Pookie had flitted in and settled on a file cabinet.

"Of course, I remember you, Doctor Watson. How could I forget? That terrible Inspector Athelney Jones had me on my way to the hangman for the murder of Lieutenant Abercrombie. You and Mister Holmes as well as Lady Juliet proved Captain Ernest Ferguson was the guilty party. As I said back then 'You were Godsends.'"

The Baroness laughed, *"And as I said back then, Yes, we were, literally."*

"How is Lady Juliet, by the way. Of course, she's in Paradise."

Juliet laughed again. *"Watson, the Major can't see or hear me but somehow knows Pookie and I are here. A unique woman of faith."*

Watson smiled. "You might be interested to know that Athelney Jones is no longer Inspector Athelney Jones. He is walking a beat in Seven Dials. A serious misstep on his part that almost got him prosecuted. I am surprised that he is still with the Metropolitan Police."

The Major sighed. "It is Unchristian to rejoice in the misfortunes of others but he is a trial. Forgive the pun. Speaking of which, Ex-Captain Ferguson has an appointment with the gallows. May God be merciful to him. But you were my saviors."

Her face wreathed in smiles, she looked at Watson and said, "I don't know how to show my gratitude to you."

The Baroness, impulsive as usual, blurted telepathically. *"Don't just sit there smiling, Doctor. Ask her!"*

Watson reacted, "In fact, Major, I am here today to take you up on that. There is something you can do for us."

"Anything within my power, Doctor. I owe you my life."

"Nothing as dire as all that." He chuckled, "Although maybe it is." He proceeded to describe the Irregulars and the Baroness' proposal to give them schooling without being at school. "They too, can be a trial. We were hoping that employing the Salvation Army's contacts and supporters, you might be able to recommend a special someone who could take on the task of tutoring them. He or she must be sympatico with our young friends and they must recognize that fact and be accepting of that person. Not easy! We would compensate the tutor appropriately. We will also be paying the urchins an additional stipend as an incentive to participate in the program. Would you be willing to assist us with our search?"

"Of course! The way you described these Street Arabs I doubt a member of the Salvation Army would be a good fit. You say there's seven boys and they are all illiterate?"

"Actually one of them is a girl but she dresses like a boy and their leader Wiggins has had some education. He needs to be treated differently."

She replied. "Let me cast about and I will be back to you shortly. I have several people in mind."

*****

The Reverend Matthew Cartwright, Rector of St. Jude's sanctuary and shelter, was both pleased and surprised to see Major Philomena Monahan enter his refuge. He would have been even more surprised if he could see the two ghosts who were invisibly tracking along unknown to her.

"Major Monahan, greetings. It's been a long time. Welcome! What brings you to St. Jude's?"

187

"Hello Reverend. I am on a mission of altruism and I could use your assistance."

"Well, as you know, our resources are quite limited but if I can share and help you, I'm only too willing."

"You are such a generous soul but I'm seeking advice and a referral for a program I am engaged in."

Juliet smiled, *"Talk about generosity, Pookie. She's taken on the project as her own."*

The dog barked and wagged her tail approvingly.

The Rector invited the Major into his office and offered tea. She graciously declined. He said, "Now tell me about this mission of altruism."

She described what she knew about the Irregulars. He, of course, was familiar with Holmes but wasn't aware of his stealthy army. "London is awash with young illiterates. But this group sounds most unusual. Are they really as clever and intelligent as you say?"

"I have it on the highest authority."

The Baroness chuckled. *"Even higher than that, eh? Pookie!"*

"They have been assisting Sherlock Holmes and Doctor Watson for several years in bringing criminals to justice. They have outmaneuvered the Metropolitan Police in many instances. But only one of them can read, write or handle numbers. We want to change that."

"We?"

"Holmes, Watson and several of his associates."

Juliet patted the dog. *"That's us, my dear! And Martha Hudson."*

"I'm in search of a tutor for them. Someone from their background they can trust and believe. They'll never enter a formal schoolroom. Given the right circumstances and the right instructor, they can be even more formidable. Do you know anyone who would fit that description?"

"Desmond O'Reilly. A clever rogue but honest and straightforward as they come. He was demobbed from the Navy. Actually well-educated but like these Irregulars, unwilling to bow down to the powers that be. He won't tolerate any nonsense from the urchins but he'll have them whipped into shape in short order. He spends some of his time here in the shelter and does odd jobs to keep the wolf from the door. He's your man. He'll be here tonight, as a matter of fact. Why don't you bring Sherlock Holmes and Doctor Watson to meet him."

"I will."

The Baroness laughed, *"Guess who else will be there, Major."*

*****

"Now, let me get this straight. You have this bunch of Street Arabs you want me to teach how to read, write and do their numbers." Desmond O'Reilly looked skeptically at Holmes, Watson and Major Monahan.

Holmes replied, "Yes, if you feel up to it. Have you tutored before?"

"I taught a few of my shipmates when I was in the Navy. It can get very dull cruising and I'm not a gambler so I ran classes in reading and writing. Not all of them stayed on but those who did made good."

189

"Excellent! The Irregulars will be a unique challenge. You will not have a captive audience like you had on your ship. I employ them to assist me in my case work. Nobody notices a scruffy urchin and that is a major advantage. They are also clever, elusive, courageous and highly intelligent. Unfortunately they are illiterate and extremely resistant to formal schooling. I already provide them with a stipend which I plan to increase if they cooperate. They have a leader named Wiggins who is a few years older and can read and write. I intend to persuade him to pressure the rest of them to participate. That is, if you are willing to handle them. You will be adequately compensated – even more so depending on how successful you are."

"Oh, I'll be successful. No bunch of street brats will triumph over Desmond O'Reilly. You bring them. I'll teach them."

Juliet was impressed. *"Pookie, this is going to be entertaining as well as worthwhile. I'm glad we talked to Mr. Sherman. I hope I can report progress to him and Raymond. The Major and the Rector are sweethearts. So is Martha Hudson. I wonder if Holmes truly appreciates what a jewel she is."*

Doctor Watson and Holmes thanked Rector Cartwright and Major Monahan for introducing them to Desmond O'Reilly. "We're calling the Irregulars together tomorrow morning. Can you join us?"

"Nothing like getting off to a quick start. I don't think you want to meet here, though. I doubt if they'd ever step inside a church or shelter. Do they have a meeting place we can use for the sessions?"

"No place definite. They float. We'll have to arrange something. Come to 221B Baker Street at nine o'clock."

"I'll be there. We're going to need books and slates."

The Major volunteered to supply them.

"I don't want to insult you, Major Monahan, but no religious tracts, please. We're going to instruct them, not convert them."

She and the Rector laughed. "Of course not! That's for later. We'll stay away until you tell us otherwise. I'll get the books and writing slates to Doctor Watson. Thank you again, Reverend and thank you, Mr. Holmes and Doctor. This is a virtuous thing you are doing."

Holmes whispered telepathically, *"And thank you, Baroness for your heavenly inspiration. You are a good soul."*

*****

" 'Ow's yer arm, Charlie?" Wiggins had just distributed their shillings plus extra 'azardous duty pay.

"It 'urts. Never been shot before. Can't say I likes it much."

"I got a signal from Mr. 'olmes. He and Doctor Watson want to see us all at Baker Street."

Simpson looked up, "Another spy job? How about Katie, George and Cashman takin' this one? Or Willie!"

The four named urchins shuffled eagerly. A chance to earn a little more coin. They hustled out of the abandoned storefront they had been occupying followed by Simpson, Charlie and Wiggins. On to 221B, banging on the door for Mrs. Hudson to admit them. Surprisingly, she smiled when she opened the entry. This set Charlie off. He looked at Simpson and muttered. "What's with the old lady? She usually goes off her chump every time we show up." They were taken further aback when she offered a plate of cookies. Not so put off as to refuse the goodies, however.

They thundered up the stairs and crowded into the sitting room. Sherlock Holmes and Doctor Watson were standing there along with a tall, heavily built man they didn't recognize. Sitting in a corner unseen was the Baroness and her dog. George looked at

191

Cashman and said. "Has Mr. 'olmes peached on us? That bloke looks like a rozzer." Cashman shrugged. They sat, knelt or sprawled on the floor looking quizzically at the detective. Wiggins took the lead. "Whatcha, Mr. 'olmes? Another caper?"

"Yes, Wiggins but of a different sort. Something the Irregulars have never done before. Let me introduce Mr. Desmond O'Reilly."

He waved at the group "Ahoy, mates!"

"Mr. O'Reilly was in the Navy."

Katie stared at him. "Were you a h'officer?"

"Not me, sweetheart. I was a simple swabbie. Wouldn't catch me with the anchor-faced brass."

The urchins laughed. All except Simpson. "So what do yer want with us?"

"A little help. I've got a special secret job to do and I need some clever young folks like you lot to give me a hand."

"That's what we do for Mr. 'olmes and the Doctor."

"Right you are but this calls for a bit of special knowledge. Whoever works with me has to be able to read, write and do sums. How many of you can do that?"

One hand went up, Wiggins.

O'Reilly looked disappointed. "I'm sorry, Mr. Holmes. I'm sure this is a clever and resourceful bunch but I need people who have those skills."

Katie, eager to participate in whatever was involved, shouted out. "Can you teach us?"

"Oh, I don't know. You'll have to be willing to work hard to get up to snuff double quick."

She jumped up and down. "I want to learn to read and write!"

O'Reilly smiled, "And do sums. What about the rest of you lads? Is the only one who wants to help me this slip of a girl."

Grumbles. "No girl is going to show me up." "What do we have to do?" "What does Wiggins say?" "Suppose Mr. 'olmes needs us." "I ain't goin' to no school."

The ex-sailor grinned. "I don't blame you. Couldn't stand school either. Because this job is confidential, I'll teach you myself. We can meet wherever you lot cast anchor. Mr. Holmes suggested you. You'll still work for him. Right, Mr. Holmes? Right, Wiggins?"

Both nodded. Wiggins was a bit dubious but decided to play along.

"All right! Are we all on board? Anybody doesn't want to play? No? Good. I'll need to get some books and slates. Doctor Watson, do you think we could get a blackboard?"

Watson nodded. The Major and Rector had seen to the necessary supplies.

Simpson, ever the skeptic, asked, "So what's this secret special job?"

O'Reilly smiled. "It's secret and it's special. You'll find out in due time after you've learned to read. We need to give you folks another name. You're Sherlock Holmes' Irregulars and you'll be O'Reilly's Readers. Does that work?"

Cheers!

"All right! We'll start tomorrow morning. We'll meet three times a week. Wiggins, you tell us where."

Holmes looked at them. "Here's an extra. Each session you attend, you earn another shilling. But you have to work for it. If you lollygag or shag off, you'll get nothing. First one to write five complete sentences that make sense, gets an additional prize. Off you go."

Thundering hooves.

Lady Juliet had been enjoying the event no end. *"That was brilliant, Holmes."*

He replied, *"Don't congratulate me, Baroness. That was all O'Reilly's idea."*

"I'm curious. What is the secret special project?"

Holmes turned to O'Reilly and asked him.

"Damned if I know. Mr. Holmes, that's your department."

*****

Three months later, Sherlock Holmes' Irregulars aka O'Reilly's Readers had progressed to the point of forming the alphabet in print and cursive, writing their full names, copying from their books and reading (slowly) from the articles contained therein. They began to form and write sentences. One or two venturesome souls even pieced out stories from one of the tabloid newspapers.

It was Katie Wilson who won the additional prize for first writing five complete sentences that made sense.

It read: *"deer mr. Holmes. here are my five sentences. I hope they make sense and win the prize. Learning to read and rite has been fun. When do we learn to do sums. Yours truely Katherine Wilson."*

Charlie, whose wounded arm had cured, got a prize for the best penmanship. Only Simpson resisted but slowly came over.

Wiggins actually helped the fledgling students and improved his own literacy in the process.

It was George who twigged to the fact that although Holmes had enlisted them in several crime fighting tasks during the period, O'Reilly said nothing further of the secret special job. " 'ere Desmond. When do we get to the secret special job you promised us?"

"Soon, George. First you also have to learn to do sums and write down your answers."

He had worked out an assignment with Holmes. An increasing number of boxes arriving on ships would never reach their destinations after leaving the docks. Two of the Irregulars/Readers were to secretly watch the traffic at the docks, count the boxes and record the names on the wagons carting them away. Holmes, O'Reilly and Watson would travel to the destinations most likely to have pieces missing and tell the rest of O'Reilly's Readers to clandestinely record the wagon loads on arrival. If there was a discrepancy, the detectives and the Metropolitan Police would move to take action to backtrack the errant shipments. As usual, nobody took notice of urchins roaming the dockyards and warehouse reception platforms. Nobody would believe they could read, write or do sums. But they could.

*****

Back in Paradise, Lady Juliet waited impatiently for word of the project's success. Three months is nothing in the afterlife but she was measuring time by London standards. "Oh, Pookie. I do so hope our young friends are using their newfound talents." The dog, who could count goals in the game of multi-dimensional fetch wasn't so sure what the fuss was all about.

Then Raymond made one of his increasingly frequent appearances. "Lady Juliet, I have news from Sherlock Holmes.

Your pet program is a resounding triumph. The Irregulars are reading, writing and doing their sums with youthful enthusiasm and using their knowledge to help fight crime. A young lady named Katherine Wilson has emerged as a star. Mr. O'Reilly is still working with them. With the Major and Rector he is opening up sessions for other Reluctant Readers."

Juliet sighed, "Wait till I tell Mr. Sherman. Thank Heaven."

"No, Thank <u>you</u>!"

Her Last Bow ?

As usual, the sun gave off a mellow glow, providing pleasant warmth on another lovely day in Paradise. Surrounded by fragrant flowers and gorgeous plants in her sumptuous orangerie, Lady Juliet Armstrong, Baroness Emeritus Crestwell, *(deceased)* sighed, setting off a series of yawns from her Bichon Frisé, Pookie. "Are you bored too, girl?"

"The Italians say, 'Dolce far niente! It's pleasant to do nothing.' Not for us! It hasn't been all that exciting around here recently. The Heavenly Theatre Guild's Saintly Spectaculars are between performances and the True Angels flight competition is finished. Even Leonardo completed his portrait of me and the choir isn't practicing anything new. I suppose we could go over to the Meadows and see Mr. Sherman and his staff. Is the multi-dimensional fetch season over since you won the championship? Don't you have other games to play or is that the extent of canine competition?" The dog yawned again.

"I wonder what is happening at Baker Street. It would be nice to see Holmes, Watson and Martha Hudson again but we have to keep our visits under control. Raymond has been very generous and helpful in allowing us to travel so let's not abuse his good nature." Pookie barked and scratched her ear causing her halo to tilt precariously.

Suddenly, a shimmering figure appeared in the door of the luxurious greenhouse. It was difficult to tell whether the individual was male or female. Tall, blond hair, in a golden robe, incredibly beautiful *(or handsome)* and smiling. "Hello Juliet! I'm Orifiel. You probably don't know me by name but I know you very well. I was your guardian angel."

197

The Baroness was shocked. (*Actually, she insisted she was never shocked. Shocking, yes, but never shocked.*) Orifiel!? My guardian angel. I always knew you were there but I never knew your name. What does it mean?"

"Gazes backward in time to view the past."

"How appropriate! Forgive me for asking. Are you male or female?"

"Neither. As you know from your angelic acquaintances, we are pure supernatural essence. The earthly artists insist on painting us like humans but we have no gender. You are made of flesh in God's image. We are spirits. Servants of the Almighty."

"Where are your wings?"

"Wings are optional. At the moment, I don't need them. Like you, I flit. May I enter?"

"Your presence is most welcome! Oh. what a delight! Don't just float there. Come in! Come in! This is Pookie."

The Bichon did a circular dance and raised her paws in the air.

"Oh, I'm well acquainted with Pookie. I remember when you got her as a tiny puppy. A present from an admirer."

"Geoffrey! That romance didn't last very long but Pookie and I stayed together for fifteen years."

"Yes, I recall how bitterly you cried when she died but I'm so glad the two of you are back together. I gather she's quite a star in the Meadows."

"And on the True Angels Aerobatic Team. She's a Canine Top Gun and Dog Fight Specialist. But it's so good to finally lay eyes on you. What brings you to my humble abode?"

Orifiel laughed. "Humble indeed. Fit for a Baroness and then some. You advanced quite a bit during your lifetime. It was a pleasure to watch over you until that fateful evening when you were shot. I'm sorry but that event was pre-ordained. There was nothing I could do to protect you. It was time."

The angel continued, "As to why I'm here. I'm between assignments. In addition to being the guardians of humans, angels are God's messengers and defenders against evil. That last role belongs primarily to the archangels. There are also the cherubim and seraphim who are engaged in constantly praising the Almighty. And no, they are not the cute little chubbies the artists insist on depicting."

"Right now, I'm on messenger duty with nothing to deliver. I decided I would seek you out. Your life on Earth was quite remarkable. Not saintly in the usual sense but remarkable. As you might imagine, your personality and mine are quite alike. Now, your afterlife has become quite extraordinary. You are legendary here in Heaven and with your associate on Earth – Sherlock Holmes. Since I'm directed to gaze backward in time and view the past, I thought we could reminisce on your mortal life and then you could tell me about your more recent memorable adventures with the Great Detective after your death."

Juliet laughed, "How delightful! And here I was bemoaning incipient boredom. I'm sure Pookie is also excited. Aren't you, girl? This beats multi-dimensional fetch. All right Orifiel, you first. Before we start, would you care for a dish of ambrosia or a cup of nectar? I believe angels can enjoy those. Some of my celestial choir companions do." She snapped her fingers and two bowls of ambrosia and two cups of nectar plus one bowl for the dog appeared. "Very convenient delivery service."

The angel smiled and took up the cup. "Thank you! Blessings on us. Where to begin? I remember a squirming, squalling bundle of noise giving her parents fits. Your mother and father were charming people. He was a solicitor. She was a librarian. Their guardian angels were quite pleased to be assigned to them and welcomed me when I was sent to you."

"Your older brother, Andrew, was quite a handful. His protector was on constant watch for his antics, falling out of trees, spraining wrists and ankles, almost drowning. And then…"

"Yes, poor Andrew. Lost in The First Boer War. You angels must have been horrified by the terrible losses in that conflict. My mother was irreconcilable. Father was "stiff, upper lip.""

"Like parents everywhere in England and the Transvaal. And now, War Number Two is on. Anyway, I recall you were something of a tomboy all through grade school, leading your little gang of urchins in all sorts of shenanigans and pranks."

She shook her head. "That's why I took so to Holmes' Street Arabs, the Baker Street Irregulars, They reminded me of me. But more of that later."

The angel smiled, "I remember your first attempt at acting in a school production. Little did we know."

"I played a church mouse. That's where I got the theatrical bug. I adored being onstage. Still do."

"I know. Many a night I spent backstage watching you in school, amateur and then professional parts. The big surprise was your amazing singing voice. I remember your mother saying you sang like an angel. I'm an angel and my singing voice is terrible. Recently, when I was no longer assigned guardian duty, I had a

200

chance to see you in the Heavenly Theatre Guild's Saintly Spectacular show -Heaven's Above. You're still sensational."

"Thank you. What happened to your last guardian assignment?"

"Cholera. He's here in Heaven."

"I'm sorry. It hurts when you're cut off early in life. I know. I originally felt frustrated on dying but I'm truly happy here and now. Of course, Raymond, Holmes and Pookie contribute greatly."

"I'm glad. I remember being very much concerned when you decided to go into professional theater."

"You mean when I took jobs as a chorus girl in the pits of sin. Those were the difficult times on the road, in fusty backwaters and in some unspeakable dives. Ugh!"

"Yet you handled them well. Not everyone does. Some girls will do anything to get ahead."

"Not this girl. I got my parts through talent and hard work-mostly hard work."

"I know. I was proud of you."

"Oh, there were the usual overly friendly producers and directors, stage-door johnnies and a few short-lived romances. That's how Pookie and I got together. At least Geoffrey was innovative enough to come up with original gifts – even if he turned out to be a swine. The dog was a blessing. Still is!"

"What was the name of the revue you first starred in? The one where you were the romantic lead and swung on a trapeze while you sang your heart out?"

"Jolly Juliet! Doesn't that take the biscuit for hackneyed titles. But my name was up in lights. And unfortunately, that's when I met the now late Reginald-Baron Crestwell. When I make mistakes, they're beauties. Reginald was a consummate fool but he was a Baron. Becoming a member of the nobility had its attractions even if the nobleman himself did not. He didn't exactly rush me off my feet. He moved and thought too slowly for that. The only thing he did rapidly was talk, mostly about himself, his influence and his formidable wealth. I believed him. When the show finally closed *(after seven hundred performances, I might add)* he proposed and I accepted. I had hoped for a luxurious honeymoon on the Riviera. Frugal Reginald decided on Margate and donkey rides. I remember thinking. 'Well, here goes my last bow.' Happily, it wasn't!"

Orifiel said, "I remember your life among the Great and Good. You were bored sick and Reginald's family was no help. Your mother-in-law was a trial. She snubbed your parents and made it clear she didn't like you."

"Hah! You spirits have wonderful memories, especially one appointed to gaze backwards. An angelic historian. Yes, the bloom was off the baronial rose rather quickly."

The angel frowned. "Unfortunately there was Selma Fairfax and her plot leading to your demise."

"Good old Selma. In spite of police stupidity, Holmes, Watson and his Irregulars tracked her down along with her hired murderers. She was hung. Speak no ill of the dead but she deserved it. The woman was a viper. But some good came of it. That's when I met Holmes."

Orifiel finished his ambrosia and washed it down with a gulp of nectar. A glassy eyed Pookie stared at the angel, gazing at his cup longingly. "Looks like our canine friend would like a refill."

"She always does. Fortunately, heavenly dogs are immune from nectar overdosing. Mr. Sherman assured me."

The angel continued. "On your death, I was assigned another protégé and lost track of your activities. I knew you were in Heaven and Raymond assured me you were active. By the way, he is ranked as an angelic Power. He didn't mention your insistence in going back to Earth to track down your killers. I heard that later. Tell me about your escapades with Sherlock Holmes."

*****

Juliet proceeded to tell Orifiel of her adventures back on Earth with the Great Detective and his associates. First her refusal to enter Heaven until her murderer was found by Holmes and brought to justice. "Poor Mr. Raymond. I am a trial to him." Of course the culprit was the aforementioned Selma Fairfax, now deceased and definitely not in Paradise.

Then her episode with the Flying Crescendos, the aerialist team whose star was killed in an act of sabotage of their equipment. Holmes uncovered the fatal illicit love affair that resulted in further deaths.

She had special praise for the virtuous Major Philomena Monahan of the Salvation Army who was accused by the idiot Inspector Athelney Jones of murdering a subordinate. Juliet, Holmes and Watson identified the true culprit. More recently, the no-longer Inspector met his comeuppance and the Major assisted in a project to enhance the lives of Holmes' urchin army, The Baker Street Irregulars.

"Here's one you'll appreciate, Orifiel. A fellow guardian angel in distress over the disappearance from Heaven of a Scottish war hero who felt he didn't deserve to be in Paradise. He was found back home after we made a trip to Hell where thankfully he wasn't

203

in residence. I got my first and hopefully only exposure to Satan. Not the least bit pleasant."

The angel shuddered. "I saw Satan and Beelzebub once at a distance. I leave it to the archangels to confront the Prince of Darkness. You have been leading an exciting afterlife."

"There's more if you're still interested."

"Absolutely. Eager to hear!"

"Well, as you know, in addition to being an excellent physician and Holmes' colleague, Doctor John Watson is a famous and prolific author. But a story he didn't write got him nearly slain."

"Then, no less a celestial celebrity than St. Patrick himself interceded to find a missing old man and his unique bass drum. He was a member of McNamara's Band of international renown. The Bishop is a lovely man and it was a pleasure to celebrate his holiday."

"Not all our adventures took place in London. A madman, intent on destroying the world by setting off volcanoes in the Pacific rim was one of the deadliest individuals we ever encountered. Nature did him in, not us."

"Another event with international consequences was a failed assassination attempt on Queen Victoria at Windsor Castle. Her Majesty has since died naturally and has gone on to her eternal reward. We haven't actually seen her but we believe she is reunited with her beloved Prince Albert here in Paradise.

"I had the delightful opportunity to work several times with Mrs. Martha Hudson, landlady to the doctor and the detective. A wonderful woman whom I really enjoy and hope to see again. Unlike most mortals, she was able to see Pookie and me. We went to the theatre and Simpson's for a wonderful dinner. Such fun! Oh, incidentally, my former husband Reginald was strangled at that same theatre. An honor killing. Oh well!

"Speaking of my canine companion, Pookie and her friends from the Meadows outside the Rainbow Bridge helped us locate a missing industrialist. Holmes' practice had gone to the dogs.

"A group of Suffragist ghosts seeking justice for one of their imprisoned number brought about a peer's and Athelney Jones' downfall."

"I already mentioned Major Monahan and the Irregulars. The street Arabs can now read and write. So, that's my story. End of adventures. We are up to date. Exit Juliet, stage left."

The angel smiled, "Not so fast! I wasn't totally frank with you. I told you I am now a messenger with nothing to deliver. Not quite true. Actually, Raymond has a message for you before you think of taking your final bow."

On cue, the Senior Director arrived with his usual outfit and demeanor floating inches above the floor. A pure spirit, he appeared as a middle-aged male, tall, dressed in morning *(mourning?)* clothes, clean shaven, not a hair out of place, dark eyes, color undetermined. He grinned *(unusual)* at Orifiel, petted Pookie and said, "Lady Juliet, I have a request from Sherlock Holmes for your services. A theatrical incident. Are you available?"

The Baroness grinned, looked at the Bichon and murmured, "Halleluiah!"

*****

"Do you think she's coming, Mr. Holmes?"

"I have a high level of confidence, Mrs. Hudson."

"I say, Holmes, what does the Baroness bring to this party?"

"Her theatrical experience, Watson. I hope she will be visible and tangible this time as she has been on several occasions in the past. She'll no doubt have the dog with her."

"Yes I do!" A contralto voice echoed as a scarlet clad phantom and white fur covered wraith shimmered into view. *"Sherlock Holmes, you called? Hello Martha, Doctor! Delighted to see you both again. Before you ask, Pookie and I can make ourselves substantial or not as required. Raymond has seen to that. Did you know he's an Angelic Power. Pretty far up in the hierarchy. And here I've been twitting him for so long."*

Mrs. Hudson clapped her hands. "Oh. it's so good to see the two of you again." She reached over and patted Pookie on the head and ruffled her ears. "Yes, you're solid. Wonderful."

The Baroness looked at Holmes. *"I just finished up a trip down memory lane with my former guardian angel, Orifiel. Never knew his or her name. They don't have genders. Pure essence. We had a wonderful time remembering my life...and death. I recalled all of our recent post mortem adventures, too. There've been quite a few, haven't there. Do you have a new one?"*

"Yes, milady. One suited to your unique talents and your dog's."

"Oh, goody. I hope it beats multi-dimensional fetch."

Quizzical looks on the faces of the mortals.

"It's Pookie's specialty. A long story. What are we doing?"

"Protecting a national traveling pageant."

"I'm sorry. I thought you said, 'protecting a national traveling pageant.'"

206

"I did. Pageantry is becoming the next great entertainment rage here in Britain. They are being held in cities, towns and open spaces; hundreds of players; thousands of spectators; subject matter celebrating history, geography, culture, drama, literature, current events, science and industry. Our client is the Royal Society for the Advancement of Automotive Machinery. They are planning an elaborate traveling spectacle. You will be called upon to play the Goddess of Motorized Marvels, under a made-up name and identity, of course. Your dog, Speedy, will be your lovable mascot. "

"I know absolutely nothing about Automotive Machinery. When Pookie and I want to travel, we fly or we flit. I hate those automajigs that are clogging London's streets. But why are you involved at all? And why are Pookie (or Speedy) and I concerned?"

"There is a group of Neo-Luddites opposed to the automobile, motor lorry and all other mechanical replacements for the horse drawn carriage, cab, wagon and dray. They have threatened to disrupt any use of mechanical road devices and are especially opposed to promotional events such as this pageant. Our job is to ferret out the leaders of the group and prevent them from carrying out their threats. Oddly enough, they have no such resistance to the railroad or water craft."

"I sympathize. I'm a horse lover. You should see the magnificent animals we have in the Meadows by the Rainbow Bridge. War horses, chargers, race horses, mounts, stallions, mares, cab, carriage and dray tuggers, ponies. Wonderful equines. But I suppose their lives will be much better once they're relieved of their weary plodding and dangerous battles. Progress is never easy."

Mrs. Hudson and Watson heartily agreed.

"So, who am I?"

207

"Madame Rose LaTour who bears an uncanny resemblance to the late, lamented star of the musical stage, Juliet Armstrong. You are to be kidnapped. If you are willing to participate, I will introduce you in the morning to Mr. Irving Pangbourne, the impresario creating this extravaganza and the members of the Royal Society's Board of Directors."

"I am to be kidnapped? Honestly, Holmes, you are too much. Explain yourself!"

"The Society has received a warning that their star chanteuse will be taken hostage and only released if the pageant is cancelled. Since you are already deceased and able to flit at will, you are the ideal captive. We want you to be abducted and then lead us and Scotland Yard to the rogues' lair where you are supposedly being held. They will never know that you cannot be confined. You can change your status from tangible to ethereal and back, can you not? The dog, too?"

"Yes! Only you could come up with an insane scheme like this. I assume Mr. Pangbourne and the Society Board will think I am flesh and blood."

"Madame Rose LaTour is a theatrical discovery of mine. You have been performing on the Continent to packed houses. I have persuaded you to come to England and join the pageant for its opening performance. The Society will then come up with another singer to finish off the tour."

She chuckled *"Let's hope no one figures out how to finish off LaTour. Pardon the pun. All right. Let's go see Mr. Pangbourne and the Board of Directors. Must I audition?"*

"A couple of rousing choruses of 'Rule Britannia' will do nicely. At the pageant, you'll be leading a crowd of thousands."

"Assuming I can escape captivity. So, we meet tomorrow morning. Meanwhile I want to catch up with Martha Hudson. Pookie, for the time being, your name is Speedy. Do you understand?"

The dog cocked her head and barked.

*****

The Royal Society for the Advancement of Automotive Machinery had its offices on the campus of the Hallman Motor Car Company. The Executive Conference Room was laid out in typical fashion with a long mahogany table flanked by comfortable chairs. Coffee and tea were available on sideboards. Already seated were the six Society Board members, the Chairman and pageant producer Irving Pangbourne. The Chairman, Mr. Rhees Hallman, was a tall, impeccably dressed, intense individual with a black forked beard, greying hair and a slight stoop. By comparison, Irving Pangbourne was short, almost rotund, flushed of complexion and sloppily dressed. The Board members were on balance nondescript.

Sherlock Holmes, Doctor Watson, Juliet and Pookie (Speedy) entered the room. The Baroness had dressed for the occasion. A silver metallic gown with scarlet trim, topped with a Union Jack sash and a silver helmet bracketed by a small set of wings in lieu of her halo. She looked like an ornament on a automobile's bonnet. Speedy wore a Union Jack ribbon around her neck.

Holmes greeted Pangbourne who in turn made the introductions to the Board members and the Chairman. They were immediately taken with Madame Rose LaTour who smiled at them and allowed the Chairman to lightly kiss her hand. Holmes presented the lady and recited her history on the Continental stage.

Hallman reacted. "I say, Mr. Holmes. Madame is 'tres charmante,' don't you know, but she is French. Hardly fitting for a British Automotive Pageant."

Juliet released her finest tinkling laugh, shook her head vehemently and said in her best theatrical Midlands accent. "Heavens no, Mr. Hallman. I'm as English as the Tower Bridge. My real name is Agatha Potts. Madame Rose LaTour is strictly for the European market. I'm sure Mr. Pangbourne can come up with a name that will fit your requirements, if necessary. Perhaps if I sang a bit for you. Her exquisite coloratura voice rang out:

> When Britain first, at Heaven's command
> Arose from out the azure main;
> This was the charter of the land,
> And guardian angels sang this strain:
> "Rule, Britannia! Britannia rule the waves:
> "Britons never will be slaves."
>
> The nations, not so blest as thee,
> Must, in their turns, to tyrants fall;
> While thou shalt flourish great and free,
> The dread and envy of them all.
> "Rule, Britannia! Britannia rule the waves:
> "Britons never will be slaves."

As expected, the men were completely gobsmacked and applauded wildly. Juliet pondered for a moment. *"Ironic that guardian angels sing that song. I'll have to check with Orifiel."*

Hallman looked at Pangbourne. "I think we've found our Goddess of Motorized Marvels. Miss Potts, it's a shame you are only available for our opening event. Can you be persuaded to stay on through the remainder of the tour?"

Holmes intervened. "I'm sorry, gentlemen, but Madame LaTour has commitments on the other side of the Channel. It took some extraordinary negotiation to make her available at all." (Little did they know about Raymond!)

Smedley, one of the Board members, guffawed. "I don't suppose your dog sings."

Watson who had been silent up to this point, said. "She does whine a bit but she is a fabulous dancer. Show them, Speedy."

The dog cocked her head enquiringly.

Juliet shifted to telepathy. *"That's you, Pookie!"*

The Bichon rose on her hind legs, pawed the air and slowly rotated while tossing her head.

More applause. Smedley laughed again. "Be careful! She's a scene stealer."

Holmes turned serious. "Indeed, we must be careful. I have warned Madame about the threat you have received from the Neo-Luddites. We are arranging to have her heavily guarded. We will not allow her to be abducted. I have great admiration for the lady. She has bravely consented to appear in spite of the warning."

Pangbourne nodded, "A real trouper!"

The Baroness chuckled to herself. *"You don't know the half of it, Irving."*

It occurred to her that she should be paid handsomely for her appearance. She must speak to Holmes. The money was going to go to the Baker Street Irregulars. A collection of good hearty meals in the offing.

Hallman frowned. "You must stop those villains, Mr. Holmes. We will not cancel the pageant. We are investing too much in this program to have it aborted. The opening event is crucial. If it is as successful as we hope it will be the tour will propel the automotive industry to new heights."

Watson thought, "To say nothing of Hallman Motors sales."

Pangbourne waved his hands. "Well, this much is settled. We have our Goddess. The site is prepared. We have a display of autos, lorries, military and farm equipment being delivered shortly. An Army band has been contracted for. Speeches by members of Parliament, the Home Office, the military and the automotive industry. Ticket sales are commencing. Special trains to the site are being negotiated."

Hallman bowed to Juliet aka Agatha Potts aka Madame Rose LaTour. He reached down and petted Pookie aka Speedy. "Madame, it has been a great pleasure. I have never heard 'Rule Britannia' sung in such a spirited fashion. I assume you will do equal justice to 'God Save the King.' "

She smiled, "Of course and I will add a song or two from the theatre. I make a lovely Bird in a Gilded Cage. Well, à bientôt, gentlemen!"

They left the building and the Baroness turned to Holmes and Watson. "Now what? Do I just stand around and wait to be kidnapped? By the way, I expect to be paid for this. Proceeds going to the Baker Street Irregulars Food Pantry administered by Major Philomena Monahan."

Watson applauded. "She will be pleased. So will Mrs. Hudson and Desmond O'Reilly. Don't forget the Rector."

Holmes nodded. "I'll see to the payment, Baroness. Query: Can you be injured in your earthly state?"

"Yes and No. I may show the consequences visibly but they have no real effect. A bruise will just disappear and nothing will break. No pains. Of course, in ethereal condition, I am totally immune from forcefulness. Are you expecting violence?"

"I'm not sure. In defending you, Watson and I may be victimized as well. We don't have any meaningful history with this group. Although I have a few ideas on who may be behind all this. Means, motive and opportunity. All on display."

Watson coughed. "What do you know about the Neo-Luddites?"

"Very little. I suspect they may not even exist."

Juliet and the Doctor stared. Pookie tilted her head.

The Baroness frowned. "I'm supposed to be kidnapped by non-existent brigands?"

"I didn't say you will not be abducted. I just don't think the Neo-Luddites will be responsible."

"You're obfuscating again, Holmes. It's irritating."

"Sorry, Milady. You know my methods by now."

"Yes and I find them annoying. Let's go back to Baker Street."

A growler turned the corner and stopped in front of them. "Cab, Guvnor?"

Before Holmes and Watson could react, Pookie jumped on board and Juliet grabbed at her. The cabbie whipped the horses and the growler took off. Juliet and her dog were being kidnapped.

The detective turned to his associate. "The game is afoot, Watson. Let us go home and await the arrival of the Baroness.

*****

The Royal Society for the Advancement of Automotive Machinery received a note hand delivered by a young lad. No return address. Printed in block letters on plain paper..

"Your Goddess of Motorized Marvels is in our hands and will not be released until a notice is published in all of the papers cancelling your national traveling pageant. Do not be deceived. We will not hesitate to harm her if you do not comply. You have twenty four hours. The Neo-Luddite Association."

Hallman transmitted the note to Holmes and Gregson at Scotland Yard with the postscript "Do something!"

Several hours passed and nothing happened. Holmes was at pains to assure Mrs. Hudson that Lady Juliet was all right. "In fact, I fear for her kidnappers. She and her dog can be quite intimidating."

Suddenly a contralto voice singing 'Rule Britannia' resonated up the stairwell accompanied by a barking dog.

"Well, here she is. Are you unharmed, Baroness."

"Yes but I'm in a hurry. They have me in a disreputable boarding house in St. Giles. I'll give you the direction. There are two toughs. One is drunk as a lord. They left me alone, tied up. You know how effective that is. Pookie ran off and hid but reappeared in her otherworldly state. I'm not sure when they'll be back but they said something about meeting the boss. Whoever that is. But that's what we want to find out, isn't it. I need to flit back. Are you coming?"

"As soon as we can. I have to summon Gregson to join us and haul in the villains."

"Are we going ahead with the pageant?"

"Perhaps, if you're willing and the Royal Society is still determined to bring it off."

She and the dog flitted back to the hovel where she set about tying herself back up.

Holmes, Watson, Gregson and a cluster of constables arrived and surrounded the St. Giles boarding house. The two toughs, quite the worse for wear from alcohol staggered back to the room past their hidden observers. "Where is he? He was supposed to pay us off after we delivered his package."

Juliet tried to get them talking. "Who are you and what do you want with me? I don't have any money but I know some people who do. Who is this 'he' you're talking about?"

"Shut up! You'll find out soon enough. Where did you get that stupid costume and where is that mutt you had with you?"

"I don't know. My dog disappeared *(literally)* and I'm sick with worry." In fact an invisible Pookie was standing next to her.

"You have more than a miserable mongrel to worry about. Wait till the boss gets here. I think I hear him now." There was a rattle at the door and a short, almost rotund, flushed of complexion and sloppily dressed individual stepped in. Irving Pangbourne! He was holding a gun.

The Baroness was surprised (But never shocked.) She prevaricated. Oh, Mr. Pangbourne. Thank goodness it's you. These men have abducted me. I think they're Neo-Luddites. Tell them to let me go."

215

The two toughs laughed. "Neo-Luddites? What are those? You have some imagination, girlie. Tell her, Boss!"

"I'm sorry, Miss Potts or is it Madame LaTour? The Neo-Luddites are a figment of my impressive imagination. It's necessary to hold you here until those idiots at the Royal Society publicly cancel that infernal pageant. When the notice is published, Irving Pangbourne will disappear and you will be released. I do hope Hallman and his crew decide not to be stubborn and insist on carrying on. You are much too talented and attractive to become a victim."

Holmes, Watson and Gregson had followed Pangbourne up to the room and were standing listening outside the flimsy door. At Holmes' signal they smashed the entrance open. Watson, with his faithful service revolver winged the armed impresario and aimed at the two stooges.

Juliet and Pookie promptly vanished.

Gregson and two constables handcuffed Pangbourne and his flunkies, read them their rights and started to push them down the stairs.

Pangbourne looked around puzzled. "Where did she go?"

Holmes laughed. "She disappeared. Wait, Inspector, let's hear what our entrepreneurial wizard has to say. Why did you invent the Neo-Luddites? Why the kidnapping and blackmail?"

"Because I'm bankrupt. I was desperate. Those bloodsuckers at the Royal Society had me over a barrel with an airtight open-ended contract. They kept adding expenses to the pageant that I couldn't afford. I had to stop it somehow. I thought I could get them to cancel if it became apparent that their star was in jeopardy. I guess they'll have to abandon it after all. All right,

Inspector. Let's go. Apologize to Miss Potts for me, Mr. Holmes. I wouldn't have hurt her."

*****

The Royal Society management felt they were too deeply committed to give up on the pageant. They hired another producer, scaled down the event but proceeded to present the wonders of automotive progress. Much to her surprise, they held the Baroness to her commitment and paid her handsomely. The Irregulars would be awash in good hot dinners for quite a while.

Needless to say (but we will anyway) the Goddess of Motorized Marvels and her dancing dog were sensations. 'Rule Britannia' was sung as it's never been sung before. In spite of their pleading and substantial financial offers the Society was unable to get Madame LaTour to sign on for more.

Back at 221B with Watson and Martha Hudson, she questioned Holmes. "How did you explain to Gregson that the kidnapping victim disappeared after the culprits had been uncovered?"

"Oh you know these flighty French women. You needed to get back to Paris."

"Paris! That's where Pookie and I want to go. The French theater, opera, and the fashion houses. Convince Raymond. You owe me one, Holmes."

About the Author

Harry DeMaio is a ***nom de plume*** of Harry B. DeMaio, successful author of several books on Information Security and Business Networks as well as the seventeen-volume ***Casebooks of Octavius Bear.*** He is also a published author of Sherlock Holmes and Solar Pons stories for Belanger Books and the MX Sherlock Holmes series. A retired business executive, former consultant, information security specialist, elected official, private pilot, disk jockey and graduate school adjunct professor, he whiles away his time traveling and writing preposterous books, articles and stories.

He has appeared on many radio and TV shows and is an accomplished, frequent public speaker.

Former New York City natives, he and his extremely patient and helpful wife, Virginia, live in Cincinnati (and several other parallel universes.) They have two sons, living in Scottsdale, Arizona and Cortlandt Manor, New York, both of whom are quite successful and quite normal, thus putting the lie to the theory that insanity is hereditary.

His e-mail is hdemaio@zoomtown.com

You can also find him on Facebook.

His website is www.octaviusbearslair.com

His books are available on Amazon, Barnes and Noble, directly from MX Publishing and Belanger Books and at other fine bookstores.